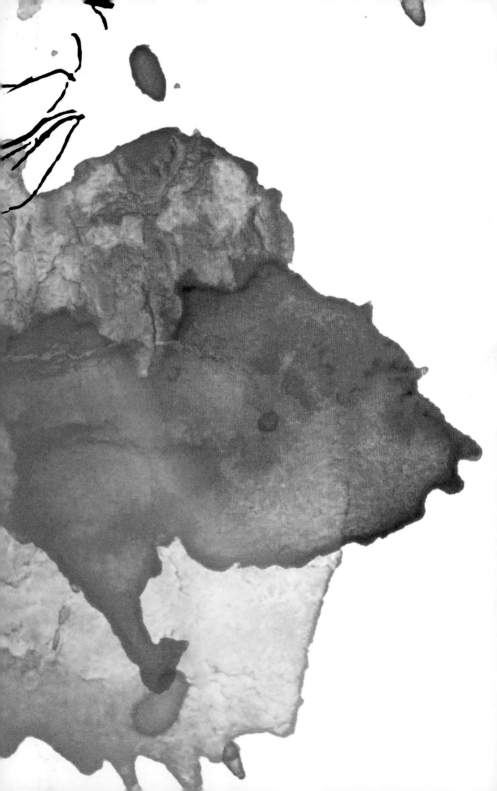

CHLOE *by* DESIGN

WITHDRAWN

Balancing Act

BY MARGARET GUREVICH

ILLUSTRATIONS BY BROOKE HAGEL

CAPSTONE YOUNG READERS
a capstone imprint

Chloe by Design is published by Capstone Young Readers
A Capstone Imprint
1710 Roe Crest Drive
North Mankato, MN 56003
www.capstoneyoungreaders.com

Library of Congress Cataloging-in-Publication Data
Gurevich, Margaret, author.
Balancing act / by Margaret Gurevich ; illustrated by Brooke Hagel.
pages cm. -- (Chloe by design)

Summary: In this collection of four previously published works, Chloe Montgomery, winner of the *Teen Design Diva* contest, embarks on her prize — an internship with a famous fashion designer in New York City.

ISBN 978-1-62370-258-8 (paper over board) -- ISBN 978-1-62370-521-3 (ebook pdf) -- ISBN 978-1-62370-566-4 (ebook)

1. Fashion design--Study and teaching (Internship)--Juvenile fiction. 2. Fashion designers--Juvenile fiction. 3. Internship programs--Juvenile fiction. 4. Mentoring in business--Juvenile fiction. 5. New York (N.Y.)--Juvenile fiction. [1. Fashion design--Fiction. 2. Internship programs--Fiction. 3. Mentoring--Fiction. 4. New York (N.Y.)--Fiction.] I. Hagel, Brooke, illustrator. II. Title. III. Series: Gurevich, Margaret. Chloe by design.
PZ7.G98146Bal 2016
813.6--dc23
[Fic]

2014046867

Designer: Alison Thiele
Editor: Alison Deering

Artistic Elements: Shutterstock

Printed in China.
032015   008865RRDF15

Measure twice, cut once
or you won't make the cut.

Dear Diary,

I can hardly believe it — I'm back in New York City! I had a quick break back home in Santa Cruz after the *Teen Design Diva* competition ended a few weeks ago, but now I'm back. Being home was fantastic. I got to spend time with my best friend, Alex, and relax with my family. And I didn't have to worry about my private moments ending up on camera for a change.

But if I thought it would be totally quiet, boy, was I wrong! A ton of newspapers and TV stations wanted to interview me. Being treated like a local celebrity was exciting, but it also made me a little uncomfortable. Even after my stint on reality TV, I'm still not totally a "look at me!" kind of girl. If it weren't for Alex encouraging me to be proud of everything I've accomplished, I might not have had the guts to do the interviews! In fact, if it weren't for Alex, I probably wouldn't have even auditioned for *Teen Design Diva* in the first place. Believe me, I know how lucky I am to have such a great friend.

Which brings me back to New York — and my internship! Starting tomorrow, I'll be working for Stefan Meyers, one of my absolute favorite designers. His style is clean, fun, and chic — exactly what I aim for with my own designs. Working for him will be amazing, but if you want to know the truth, I'm also crazy nervous. I just hope the other interns are more like Derek, one of the nicest designers from *Teen Design Diva*, than Nina, my number-one rival from back home. If they're anything like Nina, I'm in trouble. Let's just say she and I do *not* get along — not on the show and not in real life.

Ugh. Back to being positive. I'm writing this from my dorm room at FIT — yes, the Fashion Institute of Technology! Pretty cool, huh? It's going to be my home for the next two months. I haven't met my suitemates yet, but the producers from *Teen Design Diva* told me they're all interns in the city too.

I don't know what to expect from the next two months, but I'm sure it's going to be amazing! I even got special permission from my high school to miss the first two weeks of school so I can help out with Fashion Week. I'll have to write a ten-page paper about my experience here, but it's totally worth it. There's so much to look forward to!

Oh! And speaking of things I'm looking forward to . . . I can't forget about Jake McKay. He's here in New York and studying fashion marketing at Parsons, my dream school. Having both him and his mom, Liesel, my former mentor, here in the city with me will make this experience that much better. Aw, Jake just texted me wishing me luck on my first day. He's so sweet. And super cute. Just saying . . .

It's getting late, but I'm too hyped up to sleep. I'll try counting outfits and see if that helps.

Xoxo — Chloe

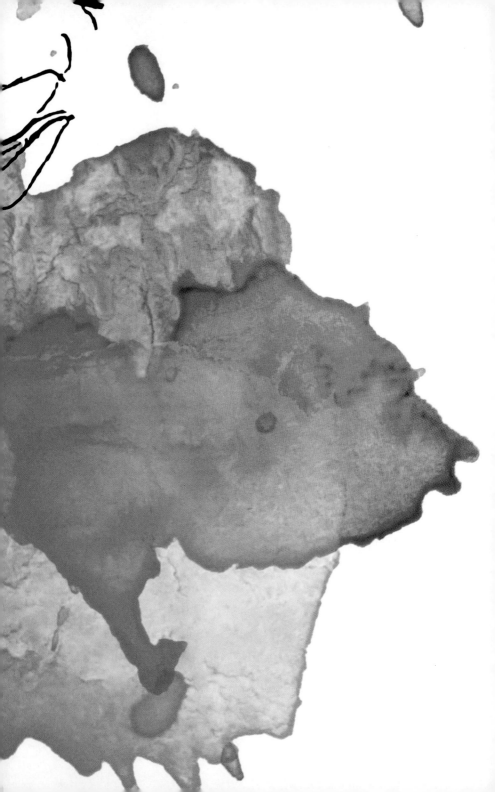

It's only seven a.m., and I still have an hour before my alarm is set to go off, but I can't fall back asleep. All I want to do is get to Stefan Meyers's office. How many times have I drooled over fashion magazines that showcased clothes from his SM label? How many times have I imagined my own initials intertwined the same way? I wonder what my first day will be like. Will I get to meet Stefan, or will he be like the mysterious wizard from Oz who hides behind a curtain?

My mind is on fast-forward as I jump out of bed. Last night I laid out the perfect first-day outfit so I'd be ready to go. Straight from my favorite Santa Cruz store, Mimi's Thrifty Threads, it's not only adorable but makes me think of home. I would have preferred to wear my own designs, but there wasn't enough time to design a whole new wardrobe before I left for New York. Mimi knows my style, and her clothes are the next best thing. Today's pick is a black sheath dress paired with red slingbacks. The shoes are a subtle accent, but *Design Diva* taught me that a pop of color can go a long way. I check my reflection in the mirror, stuff my sketchpad into my bag, and head out to the busy streets of NYC.

In Santa Cruz the streets are dead at this time. But New York City is a different world. Here, there are hundreds of people getting ready to start their day. Some are yelling for taxis, while others are enjoying the walk to their offices. During the *Teen Design Diva* competition, I felt like I was a part of the city but not in the same way. Back then, I was always rushing from one task to the next. Now, I blend in.

I stop at Starbucks and order a coffee. I have plenty of time before I'm supposed to report for my first day and decide to text Alex while I wait.

"Guess who's a working girl waiting for her morning cup of joe?" I write.

A few minutes later my phone buzzes. "Guess who wishes her phone didn't wake her up at this crazy hour?" Alex writes back with a wink face.

Oops. I forgot about the time difference between New York and California — it's not even five a.m. there. "Sorry!" I text back.

"No worries. Good luck on your first day! Tell me everything!" Alex writes as I get my latte.

I still have an hour to kill before I have to be at Stefan Meyers — I don't start work until nine — so I sit on a leather couch in the corner and take out my sketchpad. I spot a girl wearing a pleated maxi skirt and start sketching. First I draw the details of her outfit, then add her long, loose side braid and armful of bangles. She barks her order for a tall, skim macchiato, and I shade in the loose piece of fabric holding her braid together.

The girl suddenly glances my way, and I tuck my sketchpad back in my bag. It's almost eight-thirty anyway, so I head down the street to the building that houses the Stefan Meyers studio and offices. From the outside, it's not clear that designing happens here. I walk into the marble lobby, and the security guard at the front desk smiles at me.

"Can I help you?" he says.

"Um, I'm working at Stefan Meyers?" My voice goes up an octave at the end, like I'm not sure I belong.

If Mr. Security notices, though, he doesn't let on. "Name?" he asks.

"Chloe Montgomery?" My voice goes up again, like I'm asking a question. *Knock it off*, I think. *You know your name!*

"Ms. Montgomery, do you know which department you're working in today?" the security guard asks.

My mind goes blank. I had a paper with all the info, and I think I left it in my room. Great start to my first day!

"She's with me, Ken," a voice says behind me.

I spin around and see a woman in her thirties watching me. She's wearing a white blouse and slim pencil skirt paired with strappy black sandals. Her blouse is wrinkled, and the skirt has a fresh coffee stain. Her black bag is hanging off one shoulder, and the lid on her coffee cup is almost off.

"Thanks, Laura," says Mr. Security — a.k.a. Ken. He gives me a badge. "Bring this with you every day, Chloe."

"Got it," I say as I follow Laura to the elevator.

"As you can see," Laura says when the doors close, "I desperately need an intern and am ecstatic you're here." Coffee spills from her cup onto the floor, and she rolls her eyes. "Not even nine, and it's already one of those days. I'm Laura Carmichael, by the way."

"Chloe Montgomery," I manage.

"Oh!" Laura exclaims, her eyes going wide. "When they told me your name, I knew it sounded familiar, and now that I see you . . . yes! You're her! I'm sure they told me. My brain, though." She shrugs. "Wait, you *are* her, right? The *Design Diva* girl?"

I laugh. Other than being frazzled, Laura seems like she'll be easy to get along with. "Yep, that's me."

I watch the buttons in the elevator light up as we climb to Stefan Meyers's headquarters. I imagine plush, red carpeting and a maze of clothes for me to navigate. Designer jeans, dresses, and tops, all complete with the Stefan Meyers logo.

"Well, I hope you're ready to work, Chloe," Laura says as the seven at the top of the elevator lights up.

My heart beats quickly. "I'm psyched to help any way I can," I say.

"That's what I'm counting on," Laura replies. And with that, the elevator lurches to a stop, and the doors finally open.

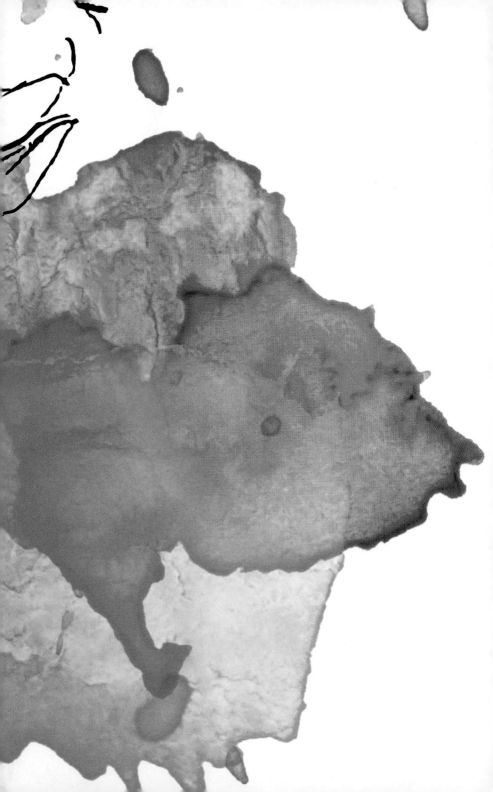

2

"Follow me," Laura says as we step out of the elevator and onto speckled gray carpet.

My heart sinks as imagination meets reality. Instead of rows of clothing and hustling designers, there's silence and drab carpeting. I follow Laura through the rows of cubicles and notice some people's eyes lighting up with recognition as I pass. I strain my neck to see what everyone is working on, but Laura is already walking into one of the nearby offices. Maybe that's where the magic happens.

I follow Laura into her office, and my mouth drops open when I see the mess inside. Design samples, fabric, and paperwork blanket her desk.

Laura laughs nervously. "Didn't I say I needed you?" she asks. "Fashion Week is less than two months away, and it's going to be completely chaotic until then."

As soon as Laura mentions Fashion Week, I perk up. I've followed Fashion Week forever. But I'd heard so many stories of interns just being asked to get coffee that I didn't want to get my hopes up about actually being involved in it.

Laura must mistake my silence for hesitation because she quickly says, "It won't be that bad, and I know this is all new to you. It can be overwhelming. But I'll walk you through everything —"

"I'm not overwhelmed!" I say quickly. "Just excited. The more involvement, the better."

Laura laughs at my enthusiasm. "Girl, you're going to wish you'd never said that."

Regret wanting to be involved in Fashion Week? No way. Not possible. The worst day in the design world is still the best day ever.

"Now that I've had a chance to drop off my stuff, let me show you around the floor," Laura says, walking back out of her office. I trail after her.

"Stefan's line covers a wide range, but his main focus for the spring line is knits, denims, and dresses," Laura explains as we walk. "Stefan is the lead designer, meaning he's the one who comes up with the vision for the pieces.

I'm the head designer for knits and denims, so he consults with me frequently. Stefan will describe what he wants, and I'll often create a sketch to match. He also does many of the sketches himself."

Laura points to a large board with different-colored fabric pinned to it. "Stefan also chooses the material, and I create prototypes of the outfits. Like these."

I lean in to take a closer look and nod in understanding. "This is to show what the outfit will look like before it's made, right?" I say.

"Exactly. We use fabrics with a similar feel to the final product, but they're cheaper. Stefan looks at the prototypes, makes the required changes, and gives the final okay to move forward to the sample," says Laura.

"What do you mean by sample?" I ask.

"Good question," Laura replies with a smile. "That's the final product of the outfit. Stefan uses the samples in fashion shows, like Fashion Week. He also presents it to buyers to show them what the label will be selling."

All around me, I see designers hard at work. Some are focused on pinning prototypes, while others are sorting scraps of fabric. I notice one woman sketching hems. "What's everyone's role here?" I ask.

"These are the junior designers," says Laura. "Sometimes they assist in a design element, but usually they're responsible for the finishing touches on a product. Embellishments, hems, stuff like that."

"When I thought of Stefan Meyers, I sort of pictured him creating everything on his own," I admit.

Laura smiles. "When I started here five years ago, I thought so too, but we all work together. Having the opportunity to collaborate with Stefan is one of the best things about a smaller label."

Laura points to a pair of designers pinning a pleated skirt on a mannequin. "That's one of the items for the spring line Stefan is going to showcase during Fashion Week. They're all trying to make sure the fit meets our original vision. Stefan will take a closer look after our weekly department meeting today."

"Stefan is coming here today?" I ask.

Laura slaps her palm to her forehead. "Sorry. I should have mentioned that. Yes, Stefan will be visiting all the departments separately today. Our meeting is at two o'clock. Next Wednesday, he's having a meeting with all the departments together."

"So I'll get to meet him?" I ask excitedly.

"Well, I'm not sure about that, but you'll be at the meeting taking notes," Laura says.

Sitting in at an actual design meeting? So cool!

Laura shows me more boards and designers adding finishing touches to garments. As more designers trickle in, it gets busier. It's finally starting to resemble what I pictured. After a while, Laura checks her watch. "Let's head back to my office. I have a big job for you before Stefan comes," she says.

I follow Laura back to her disaster of an office. I know my room back home gets messy, but this is on another level. It's hard to tear my eyes away from her apocalypse of a desk.

"Unfortunately," Laura says, following my gaze, "that's not the project. The fashion closet is an even bigger disaster. It needs to be organized so I know if it holds anything useful for the designs I'm currently working on. You up for the task?"

She doesn't wait for my reply and leads me down the hall. "Don't be scared, okay?" she says, pushing open a door.

I laugh, but stop the second I see what's on the other side of the door. The fashion closet is the size of a small bedroom, and there are piles of clothes everywhere. All adorned with the Stefan Meyers logo.

"I need you to sort the clothes by type," Laura explains. "Dresses in one section, tops in another, pants in a third, and so forth. It will probably take a few hours."

A few hours? A few days? Either way, it doesn't scare me. If Laura weren't watching, I'd dive headfirst into the pile. This closet is exactly how I envisioned my internship. Let the sorting begin!

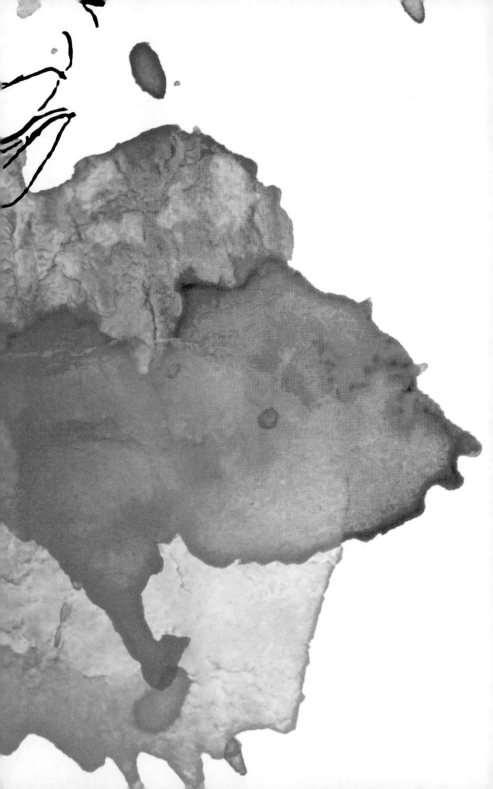

3

Two hours later, I'm still sorting. It's almost impossible to see the results, but the mountains of clothes don't bother me. Not when my fingers constantly brush pure silk and soft velvet. I spot a beige lace skirt I saw in *Fashion Weekly* and hang it near the other skirts I've already unearthed. The sheer blouse beside it joins a ruffled, cream-colored tank on the hanging rack of tops.

Just then, Laura reappears. "You got a lot done!" she says, sounding impressed as she makes her way into the closet.

I laugh. "How can you tell?"

"Trust me," she says. "At least there's a walking path now." Laura glances at her iPhone. "Our meeting with

Stefan is in two hours. I think you'll be almost done by then. Keep going. You're doing great!"

Laura heads back to her office, and my heart sinks. Two more hours of sorting is the best-case scenario. I lean against the wall, just becoming aware of a dull ache in the small of my back. Who knew organizing clothes could be so exhausting? I take a picture of the mess at my feet. "Clothing avalanche," I text to Jake before diving back into the piles.

An angora sweater tickles my nose. Sore back or not, this is still awesome. I add the sweater to a row of similar ones toward the back of the closet and move on to a pile of dresses. Just then my phone buzzes.

"Agh! Hurry and take cover!" Jake texts. "You'll be buried alive!"

I start to text him back, but Laura bursts in. "The meeting was moved up! We have to go now!" she says, thrusting a notebook into my hands and rushing back out the door.

I hurry after her. I can't believe I get to attend a design meeting on my first day! I have so many questions: What will it be like? What will they discuss? Will I even recognize Stefan? The last question makes me panic. For everything I've heard about the label, I realize I have no clue what the man looks like!

"Laura ——" I start to say.

"Here we are," she interrupts, not giving me a chance to finish.

Here is a conference room with a large rectangular table and twenty people seated around it. All of them are dressed in black — from head to toe. I take a seat beside Laura, suddenly feeling self-conscious about my red slingbacks.

"Nice shoes," says a girl next to me. She looks like she's about my age. "Love the red."

"Thanks!" I smile, feeling silly about my lack of confidence. I wonder if she's an intern too.

Just then, the room goes silent as a man in a white shirt and gray slacks enters. This has to be Stefan Meyers! His black hair is slicked back, and I can see his brown eyes through his wire-rimmed glasses. Despite wrinkles around his mouth and on his forehead, he looks young.

"I know we have several new interns starting today, so for those of you who don't know me, I'm Stefan Meyers," he says. Around the room, I see a few people sit up straighter. They don't look much older than me, so I assume they're interns too. Stefan continues, "Unfortunately, there's no time to go around and introduce yourselves right now, but please feel free to say hello after the meeting."

I make a mental note to work up the guts to go talk to him later.

"Very well, then," he continues. "As I'm sure everyone knows, Fashion Week is less than two months away. That's what we'll be eating, breathing, and sleeping until then. The items we'll be showcasing are completed or close to it. However, I did want to add two more design elements to the mix. It's crunch time, so I hope you read my latest e-mail with all the information."

The panicked faces around the table tell me they haven't read the e-mail. I write "e-mail?" in the margin of my notebook as Stefan begins a PowerPoint presentation outlining his ideas. He shows slides of skirts, dresses, and pants, all in varying lengths. I like that he doesn't just have the typical spring pastels in his color scheme. Many of the hues he presents are deeper shades of these.

I glance around the room and wonder what I'm supposed to be writing down. Will we be showcasing all of these pieces during Fashion Week?

Stefan finally turns off the screen and looks expectantly at the group. "Thoughts?"

Everyone shouts out ideas, pushing their drawings to the forefront. Only the interns are quiet. I quickly write the things I hear.

"I say tank dresses are the way to go," says someone on the other side of the room. "Maybe something with a gathered waist."

"I like that," another designer adds, nodding in agreement. "What about a pleated skirt to help give it some movement as well?"

"So, are we for sure nixing all pastels, then?" someone else calls out.

"I'm envisioning a sleeveless top with an embellished collar," a man chimes in.

I can't keep track of who's talking, but I do my best to record the ideas, taking notes and making some quick sketches. I can add details later, but at least this way I'll have some way to visualize what everyone is saying.

Next to me, Laura is quiet. She's fiddling with the designs in her portfolio, and I wonder why she doesn't shout out like the rest of the designers. Doesn't a head designer's opinion matter most?

By the time Stefan raises his hand for silence I have more than five pages of notes. "This has been very helpful," he says. "Expect a more refined plan by the end of the week."

I grab my notebook and wait for Laura, but she motions for me to go on ahead. "I need to run some things by Stefan," she says.

"Sure," I say. I head back to the closet of clothes, realizing then that I didn't say one word to the man who designed them.

TANK DRESS
DEVELOPMENT
Sketches

CM SM

LONG OR
SHORT?

EMBELLISHED COLLARS

DOODLES
AND
Ideas

SLEEVELESS
TOPS

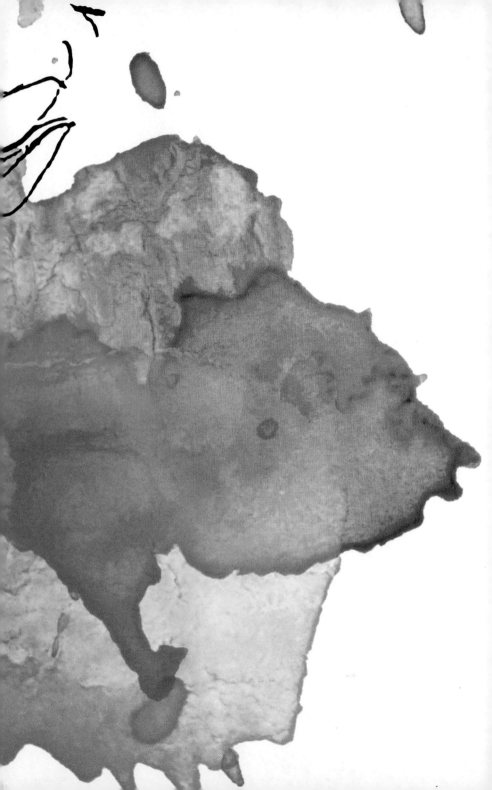

It's after six o'clock by the time I finally make it back to my FIT dorm room. I'm starving, but the thought of walking somewhere makes me want to collapse. My back is killing me after a full day of sorting clothes. Hopefully, tomorrow will involve some in-my-seat designing.

As I get closer to my room, I hear voices and remember I'll meet my suitemates today. I plaster a smile on my face and walk in. There are three girls sitting at the table in our suite's common area.

"Hey!" one of the girls says. Her reddish-brown hair is swept up with a sparkly comb. "Pizza?" She scoots over, revealing a pizza box.

I take a seat beside her and two other girls and grab a slice. "Thanks! I so didn't want to go back out." I take a huge bite.

"I don't blame you," the girl says with a laugh. "I'm Bailey." She points to her left. "This is Avery. And next to her is Madison."

My mouth is full of food, so I wave. "Chloe," I manage when I'm done chewing.

"Which designer are you interning for? Have you done it before? What department are you in?" Avery hits me with a string of questions. "Sorry. I love hearing about what everyone is doing."

"Um, I'm with Stefan Meyers?" I say. "Doing clothing design. And I, uh, this is my first internship. I won it . . ." Geez, Chloe, can you sound any more insecure?

Bailey's eyes go wide. "Hold up. You're the girl who won *Teen Design Diva*! I thought you looked familiar!"

Avery jumps up. "OMG! That's awesome! When Nina took your seam ripper I almost died. By the way, I loved your final design. The dress with the removable collar and peplum was so cute."

I blush but remember the moment proudly. "Thanks," I say. This time my voice is more confident.

"I'm psyched to intern in New York again," says Bailey. "I'm majoring in fashion design at Florida U, but one of my professors has connections here."

"You guys have all done internships before?" I ask my roommates.

Bailey nods. "Yeah, I was with Stefan Meyers my senior year of high school," she says. "They had me in dresses with Taylor, knits with Laura, and PR with Michael." She waves her hand. "I was all over the place."

All over the place? "You mean you don't just stay with one department?" I ask.

"Usually not," says Bailey. "It can get overwhelming, but the more you know about the industry, the better. You wouldn't want to have your own label and have no clue how it's run, right?" She smiles.

"Good point," I say, but the thought of moving from one department to another makes me a little nervous. I'm not sure I want to learn about PR or something like that. I already know designing is my thing. "So who are you with now?"

"Mallory Kane," says Bailey. "The woman is brilliant, but she's just as kooky as she seemed on television. She still gushes about the emerald-green dress you sewed when she was a guest judge."

"You're famous, girl!" says Avery.

"As if," I say, laughing. It's then I realize Madison has not spoken since I came in. I turn toward her. "How about you?"

"This is my first internship," she says. "I'm with Stefan Meyers too."

"Really? I'm surprised I didn't see you at today's meeting."

"Unless there's an all-company meeting, we don't usually see the other interns from other departments. I'm in dresses with Taylor," she says.

"Cool! Do you love it?"

Madison shrugs and focuses her attention on her pizza. "I don't know. Taylor's kind of uptight."

"Taylor's okay," Bailey chimes in. "I worked with her when I was interning at Stefan Meyers. I think she just takes her job really seriously. Being the head designer for all of dresses is a lot of responsibility."

Madison shrugs again. "I guess. We had our meeting with Stefan today, and I didn't get a chance to voice my ideas at all."

Avery laughs. "That's because we're interns! We'll be lucky if the junior designers even know our names. Let alone the head of the whole label."

I think back to our meeting with Stefan — everyone was trying to show him their drawings. "Yeah, during our meeting, everyone wanted to be noticed," I say. "I just took notes."

Bailey nods and laughs. "Yup. That's how it is. I mean, you have the head designer, the junior designers, the design assistants . . . *everyone* wants to move up."

"Whatever," Madison mumbles. "Not all of us can have our internships handed to us."

My skin gets hot. Is she talking about me? "No one handed me anything," I say firmly. "I worked really hard to get here."

Bailey and Avery shift uncomfortably.

"No offense," says Madison with a little smirk. "I just meant some of the other designers were better. Like Nina LeFleur."

"C'mon, guys," says Avery softly.

I shake my head. "It's fine," I say, then turn to Madison. "You're right, the other designers *were* amazing. Lucky for me, though, you weren't one of the judges."

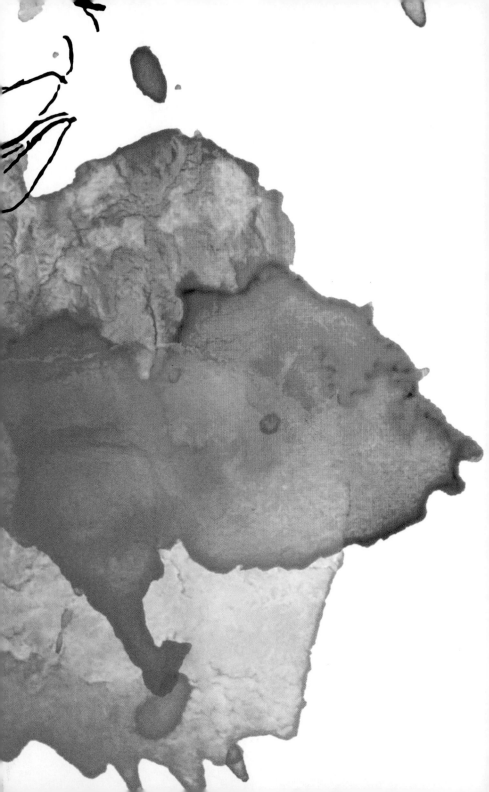

5

On Tuesday, I wake up early again and head straight to the office. I don't want to hang around my dorm longer than necessary. Madison clearly doesn't like me, and I have no idea why. Maybe she tried out for *Teen Design Diva* and didn't make the cut, or maybe she really did hate my designs. Who knows.

I learned my lesson the other day and know it's too early to call my mom thanks to the time difference. Instead, I have to settle for imagining a conversation with her. I'm sure she'd tell me that the world is full of different people, and my job is to be the best version of myself. That's the kind of thing she always told me when Nina and I were going head-to-head.

I'll be honest . . . I love being here, but I really miss my mom. It was great having her here during the *Teen Design Diva* competition, but the show paid for our accommodations. My housing at FIT is covered during my internship, but my mom couldn't afford to stay in NYC for the rest of the summer. We text or call each other every day, and I try to focus on the positive, but it's hard without her here.

I think about texting Alex and filling her in on Madison, but I know what she'd say too. I can hear her voice in my head: "Don't let the haters get you down, Chloe." Both she and my mom would be right, but logic and feelings don't always go together.

When I arrive at work at seven-thirty, the security guard sees my badge and waves me forward. I take the elevator straight up to the seventh floor and head to Laura's office.

Laura grins when she sees me. "I love that you're here early. It shows me that you're motivated."

"I am," I say, sneaking a glance down the hall toward the fashion closet. My back still hurts. I hope there aren't new piles.

Laura follows my glance and laughs. "Don't worry. The closet is done. Today, I need help assembling patterns for Stefan."

"I love designing," I blurt out. I immediately feel silly. *Duh, Chloe*, I think. *Everyone here loves designing. That's why they work for a designer.*

Laura smiles. "That's great," she says, "but this is probably a little different from what you're used to. As you heard at the meeting, Stefan is going to send out his detailed plan by the end of the week. When I talked with him after the meeting yesterday, he gave me some ideas about the direction he's leaning. He's asking several departments to create boards like the ones I showed you yesterday during our mini-tour. Remember them?"

I nod. "Will I get to help with those?" I ask. It would be so cool to contribute to Fashion Week in some small way.

"That's what I'm counting on," Laura says. "You're going to work with me to create mini-designs to pin up. Then Stefan can review them and decide which ones best represent his vision. He'll use what we created to further develop his designs, and we'll hear more of his thoughts at next Wednesday's meeting."

"But there are so many designers," I reply. "He can't like *all* our designs!"

Laura laughs. "True. And sometimes he doesn't like *any* of them. Trust me, I've seen it happen. Stefan is very talented, but it can take a lot of back-and-forth discussions to get a garment just right. Like, he may *think* yellow silk will look perfect paired with pink cotton . . . but after he sees it, he may decide the design needs to be changed."

My face falls. We could make a whole board of ideas, and it could all be for nothing. "That's a lot of work for no reason."

"I felt like that when I started too," Laura agrees, "but I get it now. Imagine if we didn't do that. We'd order fabric, start working on a design, and wouldn't realize until the end that something didn't work. This way saves time in the long run."

I nod. Laura's right. That does make more sense.

"So we do samples," Laura continues. "Stefan may be hesitant about a pattern's selling potential, but when buyers express a lot of interest in something, it shows him he's on the right track. Or, he may love a design, but when it tanks with buyers, that shows him he needs to change his plans."

I'm starting to realize that there's still *a lot* I don't know about this industry. Imagine putting your heart and soul into a design only to have others hate it.

Laura looks at her phone. "We need to get moving. Pockets are one of Stefan's focuses, so I'll need you to create samples of them."

Pockets are simple to make, but there are so many variations. Still, I think I can handle that. "What kind?" I ask.

"Stefan wants to expand his denim line," Laura says as she rummages through the mess.

"How about working with embellishments?" I suggest, already picturing the possibilities. "We can create borders of embroidered flowers or lace trim. Or pseudo-pockets with a satin border?" I think of the final *Teen Design Diva* challenge, when Derek created pants pockets that were only visible inside the garment. "Or hidden pockets so the outfit won't look bulky?"

"Here they are!" Laura finally exclaims. She pulls a stack of papers from the corner of her desk.

Maybe when we're done with the pockets, I can organize Laura's desk, I think.

"You and I are on the same page, Chloe," Laura continues. "Come check out these sketches."

I lean over and look at Laura's drawings. She has sketches of flowered pockets, embellished pockets, hidden pockets, contrast stitching, and more. I beam, feeling proud that my vision was so close to hers. I might have a lot to learn, but I'm on the right track.

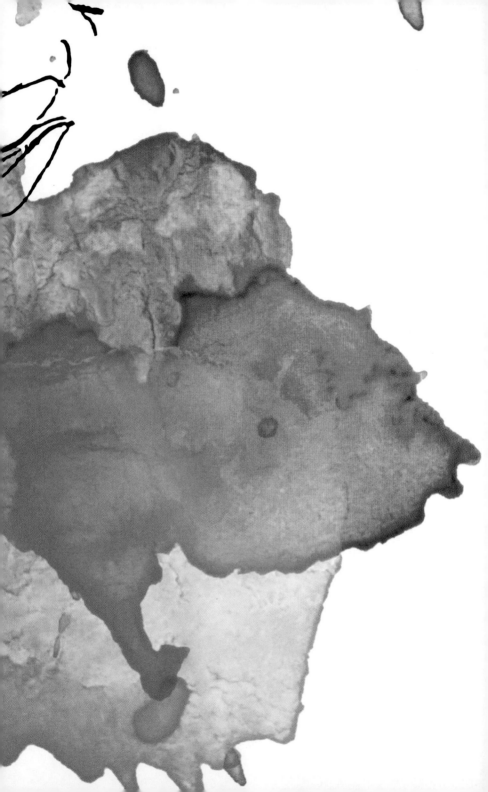

At the end of the day, I decide to stop by Liesel's store. I thought I'd see her all the time since we're both in New York, but I haven't seen her since the *Teen Design Diva* finale. When I walk in, she's helping a customer and doesn't see me. I let her do her thing.

"That's perfection," I hear her say as she pairs a soft-looking scarf with an elegant maxi dress. The customer grins. I love seeing how the right outfit can brighten someone's day.

As the customer leaves, Liesel notices me standing near the front entrance and rushes to meet me. "Chloe!" she says, giving me a big hug. "What a wonderful surprise!"

"I hope it's okay that I just popped in," I say.

LIESEL McKAY Design

SOFT PRINTED SCARF

PRINTED FLOWY FABRIC

ELEGANT MAXI DRESS

"Of course!" Liesel exclaims. "Let me look at you!" She steps back, giving me the once-over as if she hasn't seen me in years.

"Liesel," I say with a laugh, "it's only been a few weeks."

"It feels longer," she says. "You seem so mature. Must be the internship." She winks at me.

"It *has* been amazing," I say. "I even got to see Stefan!"

"Oh, that's right," says Liesel. "I heard you were at Stefan Meyers." She moves over to the scarves and motions for me to follow. She begins folding the lightweight scarves, organizing them by color. "I helped them with their fall line last year, and we're finalizing details for the spring line too. I'll keep you posted. Who are you reporting to?"

"Um, Laura Carmichael. She seems really nice. Right now, we're working on pocket embellishments," I say, folding a patterned scarf and adding it to Liesel's growing pile.

"Laura's a sweetheart," Liesel agrees. "Smart too. I've been in meetings with her. She always seems a little quiet, but I think she's just taking it all in and waiting for the right time to voice her opinion."

I think back to yesterday's meeting. Is that what Laura was doing? "We actually had a meeting yesterday," I tell Liesel. "A lot of the other designers were yelling at Stefan and almost fighting each other to show off their designs.

Laura just kind of sat there, which I was a little surprised by. I mean, she's a head designer, too."

Liesel looks up from the scarves. "Do you think Stefan remembered everything the others shouted at him? Do you think he could even hear who said what?"

I know I had a hard time hearing what was going on. "Probably not?"

Liesel nods. "Most definitely not. I'm sure he heard the gist, but specifics?" She shakes her head. "I bet Laura stayed after the meeting and talked to him. That's what I would have done. It's easier to get a sense of what a designer wants one-on-one."

"She did stay after!" I say.

"See," Liesel says. "I know Laura might not come off as the most organized, but when it comes to getting the product right, she gets all the information she needs to do a good job. She also knows it's about creating something for the Stefan Meyers brand, not about Laura Carmichael getting the spotlight."

Liesel looks at me pointedly like I'm supposed to read between the lines of this conversation. I nod like I get it, even though I don't.

Just then, a herd of customers bursts through the doors, and Liesel smiles a welcome.

"I'll let you work," I say.

Liesel hugs me goodbye. "Let's do lunch next Tuesday. Jake or I will text you about it. It was great seeing you!"

As I leave Liesel's store, I realize how thankful I am to have her. It softens the blow of not having my mom nearby.

My stomach growls on the way back to the dorms, and I stop to buy a soft pretzel from a street vendor. I'm immediately reminded of Jake. During *Teen Design Diva*, when I was feeling really discouraged, Jake and I had a great talk about what I wanted. He made me see that giving up wasn't the answer. Then, he bought me a soft pretzel and took a picture of me with mustard on my nose.

Smiling at the memory, I put a dab of mustard on my finger and place a drop on my nose. Then I snap a photo with my phone and send it to Jake. "Missing our talks," I write.

A minute later, my phone buzzes with a text. A photo of Jake, burger in hand and ketchup on his nose, pops up on the screen. "Miss you too!" he writes. "Hang on Friday?"

"That would be great!" I write back.

I'm so excited! This will be the first time I've seen Jake since I've been back in New York. I want to turn cartwheels, but my stomach growls again. As if on cue, my phone buzzes with a text from Bailey. "Hurry up and get back to the room before all the Chinese food is gone!" it says.

Looks like intern dinner is going to be a tradition! I think as I pick up my pace.

"It's about time!" Avery says when I get to our room ten minutes later. "It's hard holding these girls off. They're like vultures!"

"Hey!" says Bailey, tossing a napkin at Avery. "I prefer to think of myself as an exotic bird."

"An exotic bird with noodles in her hair," I say, laughing.

Bailey and Avery crack up, and even Madison smiles a little — I think.

"How was your day?" asks Bailey.

"Good! Laura has me working on pockets," I tell her. "It's super cool figuring out all the different ways to make each one stand out. How about you?"

"Mallory has us doing prototypes of sleeves," Bailey replies. "Like you said, it's impressive how unique each design can be."

Avery nods. "I feel the same way about the bags. I never noticed what goes into making a clasp. I'm going to be paying more attention to my purse from now on!"

Madison picks at her food. We didn't start off on the best foot, but I try again. "How's it going in dresses?" I ask.

"Boring. Taylor is having me make prototypes of collars." Madison rolls her eyes. "That's hardly noteworthy."

"It's kind of like with sleeves and pockets," I say, trying to be positive. "They might seem small, but a garment wouldn't be the same without them."

"Whatever. I'm better than that," says Madison.

Out of the corner of my eye, I see Bailey raise her eyebrows. Even though I'm sure she meant that as an insult to me, it sounded like Madison was dissing all of us.

"Can't be famous in a day," says Bailey.

Madison snorts. "Tell that to Miss *Design Diva*. Kind of got famous pretty quickly, huh?"

I'm too shocked to even respond. By the time I think to open my mouth, Madison has retreated to her room and slammed the door.

"Wow," says Avery. "What crawled into her bonnet?"

"What?" I say, giggling. "I've never heard that expression."

Avery blushes. "My grams says that all the time. It's sort of like 'what's her problem?'"

Bailey laughs. "I get it, but it sounds so old-fashioned." She repeats the phrase in a funny accent, and Avery and I crack up.

The rest of the night, whenever there's a lull in conversation, one of us says, "Did something crawl into your bonnet?" and we all start cracking up.

When I go to bed, I'm thankful for roommates like Avery and Bailey, but hope Madison warms up too. Dealing with mean girl Nina during *Teen Design Diva* wasn't fun, but it would have been *a lot* worse if we'd had to room together.

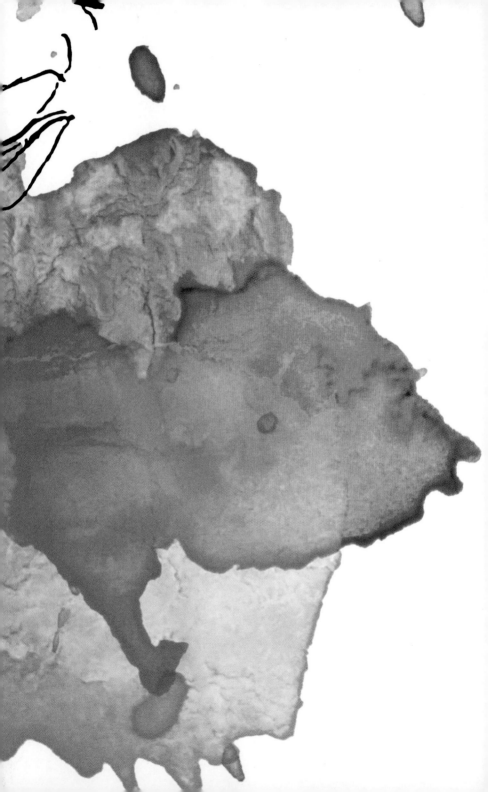

7

On Thursday, I'm still working on pockets. Two full days of pockets might sound boring, but it's amazing how creative I can get. Even though pockets are such a tiny part of the whole outfit, the little details on them can make a piece pop. It's fun thinking of how to set each one apart.

With each prototype, I check Laura's designs, then recreate them on the fabric by hand or machine. Laura has been great about letting me add my own flair to the designs. For example, one of her sketches was of a pocket with embroidered pink flowers. I tweaked the design by choosing darker shades of pink and adding a small pearl in between each flower. Laura loved it.

Sometimes I have to run to other departments for a piece of fabric or a sketch, and it's so interesting to see how other designers work. A lot of them design on the computer. I like that my department is hands-on, and I can sew my prototypes. How do you get the same feel for the garment if you're just pressing computer keys?

Later that morning, Laura stops in to check on my progress. "How's it going?" she asks as I pin a black denim pocket with lavender trim onto the board.

I step back and look at the designs. "Pretty good."

Laura nods. "I think so too. That black pocket is different. I wouldn't have pictured it in a spring line because it's so dark, but the lavender trim is the perfect accent. She steps closer to it. "Hmm . . . that gives me an idea for a dress. Maybe we could flip it — a lavender dress with black trim."

Laura's enthusiasm makes me feel good, especially since I've still been stewing over Madison's rude comments. I'm trying not to let her get to me — sticks and stones and all that — but every time she gives me a mean look or mumbles something under her breath when I walk into the room, my confidence is shaken.

Take this morning for example. I was feeling awesome in my outfit — a black dress paired with a striped scarf and gold flats. Then, as we were all waiting for the elevator, I saw Madison point at me and whisper something to another intern. I began to second-guess myself almost immediately.

I've been texting with Liesel and Jake, but I'm keeping this mean girl drama on the DL. I don't want them thinking I can't handle myself here. Whenever the nastiness starts to get me down, I focus on seeing Jake tomorrow and perk up.

"What do you think of this, Chloe?" Laura asks when she emerges from her office an hour later. I look at her sketch and am awed. In no time at all, she's made a sketch of the dress she mentioned. It has a scalloped V-neck and hem and is accented with a lavender border.

"How did you do that so quickly?" I ask.

Laura blushes. "Practice, my dear."

"The border and neckline make it look so fun!" I tell her.

"Thanks," says Laura. "We're a good team. Your pocket really put this idea into my head."

I blush happily. *Who would have thought something as small as a pocket could be a stepping-stone for an entire design?*

Laura glances at the clock on the wall, and I do the same. It's almost noon. Time passes so quickly here. "I think we've worked hard enough this morning," she says. "Take a break, and I'll see you after lunch."

I practically skip to the elevator. I can't wait to see Jake tomorrow and tell him about my week, especially today. I think of Laura's dress and how amazing it would be if Stefan picked that design. Knowing I played a part in its creation feels so good.

Personal Style:
Flair
& Details

PAINTED
EMBELLISHMENT

SATIN
PIPING

GOLD STITCHED PATTERN

STUDDED
EMBELLISHMENT

ROSE
APPLIQU

POCKET
PROTOTYPE
Sketches

I get in line at Starbucks, grabbing a pre-made sandwich for lunch. All around me, New York bustles. I love everything about this city. I could so see myself living here. When I started the *Teen Design Diva* competition at the beginning of the summer, the city was intimidating, the streets too crowded, and the subways too confusing. I missed the calm of Santa Cruz. Now, more than a month later, I feel like I'm fitting in. Of course, I miss my friends and family, but it's amazing to realize how far I've come.

"Next!" yells the barista.

I put my sandwich on the counter. "A caramel macchiato too, please."

I pay for my order and step aside as the machines puff and sputter. More people flood in, and I hear a familiar voice complain about the line — Madison. I don't think she's spotted me, and I cross my fingers that my drink will be ready soon. I don't need her killing my good mood.

"Talk about a long day!" Madison says loudly to someone beside her. "If I have to make one more collar, I'm going to throw up."

"I spent all morning sketching clasps and zippers," the girl with her replies. "It's not Paris runway, but I like it."

I recognize the voice as Avery's and almost turn around, but something stops me.

"Maybe it's easier where you are," Madison grumbles.

"I don't know," says Avery. "Isn't Chloe at Stefan Meyers too? She seems really happy there."

"Whatever," says Madison. "First of all, she's not with Taylor. And second of all, I bet they take it easy on her."

"C'mon, Madison. Don't be like that. It sounds like she's working really hard."

I stand on my tiptoes and see Madison toss her hair over her shoulder. "Sure, she makes it *sound* like that. But she'll say anything. And I'm not the only one who feels like that."

Avery shifts her feet and turns away from Madison, but Madison keeps talking, her voice getting louder. People in the coffee shop are starting to turn and listen.

"No one expects her to do well," Madison continues. "This is all promo. She won this gig on *Design Diva*, so of course Stefan has to follow through. Everyone is just waiting for her time to run out so he can get a real intern who has a clue."

Tears spring to my eyes. *Is that true? Was Laura just humoring me this morning? Did Stefan tell her to make me feel important so I'd give a good report about my experience?*

Just then, a barista shouts, "Caramel macchiato for Chloe!"

I grab my drink and sandwich and run out the door, not stopping to see Madison's reaction. All I want to do is get away from Madison and anyone else who feels the same way she does.

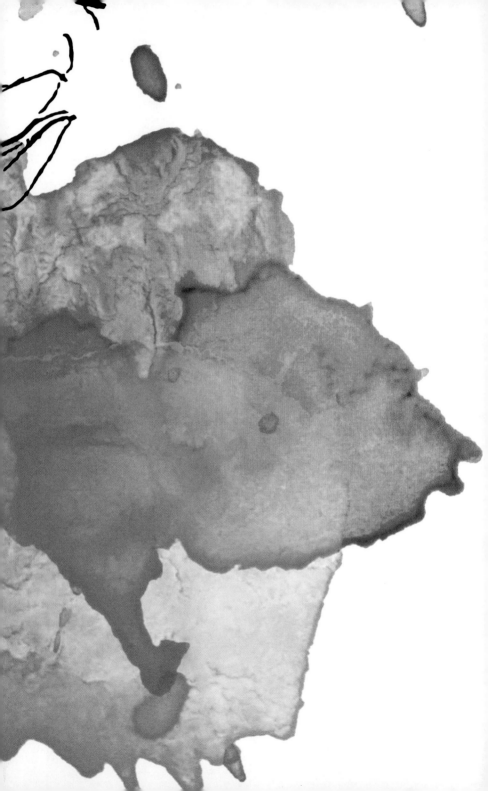

8

It's finally Friday! I felt like it would never get here. After I went back to work yesterday, I was totally distracted. I couldn't stop thinking about what Madison said. Seeing Jake today will be terrific, and any time away from Madison is an added bonus.

Jake and I have plans to meet up after I'm done for the day. Our first stop is the Ripley's Believe It or Not! museum in Times Square, which Jake said is a "total must-see."

When I arrive and see him standing at the entrance, it's all I can do not to run to him. I'm glad he's less reserved. As soon as I'm close enough, Jake grabs me and twirls me around. Then he gives me a kiss on the cheek. "It's so good to finally see you," he says, still hugging me. "Much better than just texting."

I laugh. "Agreed." He puts me down and brushes the hair from my eyes.

Jake and I hold hands, and he gives mine a squeeze as we walk into the museum. The first thing we see is an upside-down faucet with water shooting upward.

"How do they do that?" I ask. I'm tempted to look it up on my phone, but decide to hold off. I'm sure this won't be the last thing that blows my mind in this place.

"Believe it . . . or not," Jake deadpans, and I laugh.

We walk farther into the museum and see photos of weird creatures like a two-headed calf and a seventeen-foot African albino giraffe. Past the giraffe, I spot a shrunken head behind glass. "Gross!" I say. "Where do they find these things?"

Jake laughs. "Gross? What great inspiration for a jewelry line! My mom has to see this!" He snaps a picture with his phone.

I make a face. "No one would wear that!"

"You'd be surprised," he says, grinning.

"For Halloween, maybe. I'd love to be there when you try to sell Liesel on this idea." I laugh.

Jake shakes his head. "Everyone's a skeptic," he says with a wink. "Just you wait and see."

We make our way to a dark tunnel illuminated by rainbow lights next. The lights fizzle and sparkle around us. "Now this," I say as we walk, "could spark a design idea."

"Maybe," Jake agrees grudgingly. "I mean, if you're into the colorful, pretty, not-disgusting angle."

"Right," I say with a laugh. "What sane person would like that?"

We crack up as we walk to the other exhibits. Exploring the weird and wonderful with Jake is exactly what I need today.

* * *

After Ripley's we head to dinner. Jake tells me about a spooky restaurant called Frankenstein's Tavern, and it sounds perfect. A full day of creepy!

"Some people believe it's really haunted," Jake tells me as we reach the restaurant's oversized wooden doors. He wiggles his eyebrows and pretends to look scared.

I roll my eyes. "I'm shaking."

The doors creak open, and a man with crazy Frankenstein hair greets us. I know he's totally safe, but I get goose bumps anyway.

"Welcome," says the man in an ominous voice. "Follow me."

He leads us through a maze of dark hallways where we're bombarded with florescent lights and random screams. We're finally seated in a corner beneath a large, very real-looking cobweb. A — hopefully — fake spider crawls above us.

"Your shrunken head design is just what this place needs," I tell Jake.

"I knew you'd finally see the brilliance of my idea!" Jake says. "Big bucks, Chloe Montgomery, big bucks."

"Yep, I can see it now," I say with a grin. "'College Student Rises to Fame With Shrunken Head Necklace Collection.'"

"Why stop there?" Jake asks. "I'm thinking about doing an entire jewelry line!"

I laugh so hard I snort and am embarrassed until Jake laughs even harder. Once we compose ourselves, we check out the menu full of gross-sounding dishes, like Missing Finger Potpie and Baked Mac and Sneeze.

"What will it be?" our waiter asks.

"Two Brains on a Stick," says Jake.

"With a side of your Curly Toed Fries," I add, trying not to gag.

"Oh, and two Quicksand smoothies," says Jake.

"I hope we don't end this date in the dungeon," I say after our waiter leaves.

"If I had to be stuck in a dungeon with anyone, I'd want it to be with you," Jake says with fake seriousness. "So, tell me more about your internship. I want to hear everything."

"Well, my boss, Laura, has been really supportive," I tell him. "And she's been open to my ideas. So that's encouraging. By the way, I saw your mom the other day, and she said she's worked with Stefan Meyers before too!"

Jake nods. "Yeah, she loves that place. Oh, that reminds me! I'm supposed to tell you that the new Stefan Meyers department is dresses. She said you'd know what she meant."

I laugh. "Yeah, she told me the other day that she's going to be working on a new spring line with Stefan but wasn't sure which department. Now she knows."

Jake shakes his head and smiles. "So like my mom. She could have just said that. Instead, I feel like a spy giving a cryptic message."

"What about you?" I ask. "How are your classes going? What's marketing like, anyway?" I realize I don't really know what that is.

"We have to come up with ways to present the designs to make them more appealing," says Jake. "A good design is key, but if the campaign to get the word out stinks, it might fall flat."

I'm not sure I get it. "But shouldn't a good design say it all?"

"Not always." Jake thinks for a few seconds, then snaps his fingers. "Here's an example I studied. A few years back, Johnny Q. created a suit that was supposed to be the next big thing in menswear."

"I love his stuff," I say. "It's fancy without being stuffy."

Jake nods. "Right. But when they were coming up with the marketing campaign, they thought it would be funny to have the tagline 'Not your grandpa's suit.' They focused a lot on old folks, and people got offended. All younger buyers remembered was some old dude wearing a suit. No one bought it. So, see? A good design is a start, but there's more to it."

"Impressive," I say. "Will you run my marketing campaign for Chloe's Cute Clothes when I'm famous?"

"With pleasure," says Jake. "We'll start by changing that name. Too long."

I laugh. "You're the expert," I say. This hangout is exactly what I needed. I'm having such a great time, it's not hard to push Madison out of my mind.

"I'm glad I'm going to see you more now that you're back in New York," Jake says, squeezing my hand. "Speaking of, my mom says you two have a lunch date on Tuesday. Mind if I tag along?"

I tap my chin, pretending to think about it. "Uh, I *guess* that would be fine."

"Gee, thanks," says Jake, acting hurt.

I playfully push my shoulder against his. "You know I'm happy to see you as much as possible."

Our waiter arrives. "Two Brains on a Stick," he says. Talk about mood kill.

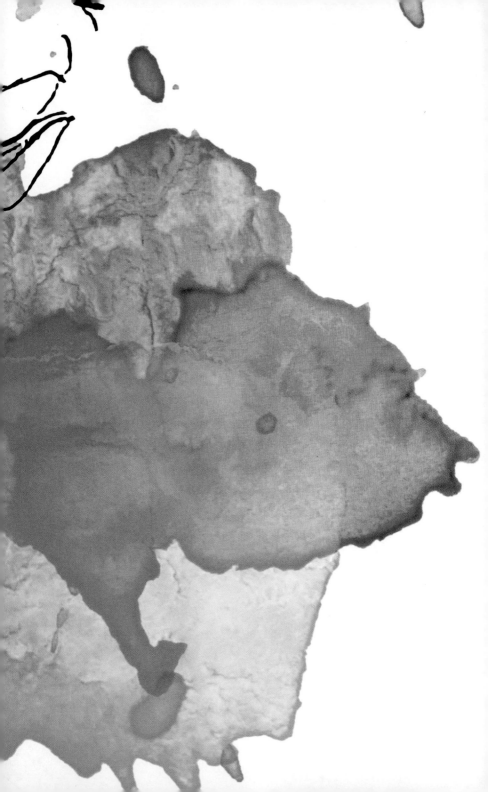

I think about the perfect Friday with Jake for the rest of the weekend. I also do my best to avoid Madison. By the time Monday rolls around, I'm ready to put what she said behind me. Despite what she said, I'm sure not *everyone* agrees with her. Avery and Bailey don't seem to. I head to the office with a good attitude, but it fades a bit when I approach the elevators, and the first person I see is Madison.

She smirks at me. "Nice bag," she says.

Today, I'm wearing a pair of cropped, ankle-length black drawstring pants with a pale peach T-shirt. I threw on a pair of gold flats to add some shine and grabbed a cool leopard-print bag to hold my sketchbook and other necessities. The outfit is very Stefan Meyers, but Madison's comment gets to me anyway. Which is probably her goal.

I want to shoot back something nasty, but the last thing I need is Madison making up stories about how rude I am. Instead, I step into the elevator, knowing she'll wait for the next one.

Laura is already at her desk when I walk into her office, and I spot two empty coffee cups in the trash. I see she's added details to the dress design from last week and is working on something new. There are prototypes strewn across the floor and spilling off the corners of her desk.

"Can I help you organize your desk?" I blurt out.

Laura looks surprised, and I realize that may have sounded impolite.

"I'm sorry," I begin. "I didn't mean —"

"No, it's okay. I would *love* that. I didn't want to ask because I know how boring organizing can be."

"I'm glad to help," I tell her.

Laura and I study the mess on her desk. She doesn't seem to know where to start, and I wouldn't want to throw out something she might need.

"Do you have any baskets or bins?" I finally ask. "I could sort things for you. Maybe receipts in one basket, fabric in another, designs in another, and so on. Then I could label each basket with tape and a Sharpie. Would that work?"

Laura's face brightens, and she opens her desk drawers. She digs for a moment, finally emerging with rolls of tape, several baskets, and a black Sharpie. "That would be a lifesaver," she says gratefully.

"Consider it handled," I say confidently.

Laura heads to a nearby conference room to continue working on her designs, and I start organizing. She's right about the task not exactly being fun, but oh, well. Laura has been so supportive of me; I want to do something nice for her too.

Besides, I think, *the more organized her desk is, the easier it will be for her to find designs. That's a win-win for everyone at Stefan Meyers.*

By the time I'm finished, it's almost lunchtime. Laura's mouth drops open when she walks in. The multi-colored baskets look great beside her desk, and the labels make everything easy to find.

Laura walks by each of the baskets and runs a hand over her empty desk. "I was beginning to forget what this thing looked like. Thank you!" she gushes.

"You're welcome!" I reply.

"I'm tempted to give you the rest of the day off," says Laura.

"No!" I exclaim. "Don't do that. I can do more." Madison's words are still stuck in the back of my mind, and I want to prove myself. I need to show Laura that I deserve to be here.

Laura laughs. "I'm glad to hear that, because I have a big job for you. There's a lot to do in preparation for Wednesday's big meeting with Stefan."

I can't believe the meeting crept up so quickly. It feels like I just started here.

Laura scans the baskets and pulls out a sheet of paper from the one labeled LISTS. "These are some things I need picked up — fabrics, findings, all kinds of things. I certainly don't expect it all done today, so don't kill yourself."

I take the list from Laura and look it over. I can find a lot of these things at Mood, and I have a pretty good idea which stores in the Garment District will have the rest. Shopping will be great.

Maybe I'll even find some stuff for my own designs, I think hopefully. Working here has been inspiring, but other than that first day at Starbucks, I've hardly had any time to sketch my own stuff.

"I'll do as much as I can," I tell Laura, but I plan to finish the list.

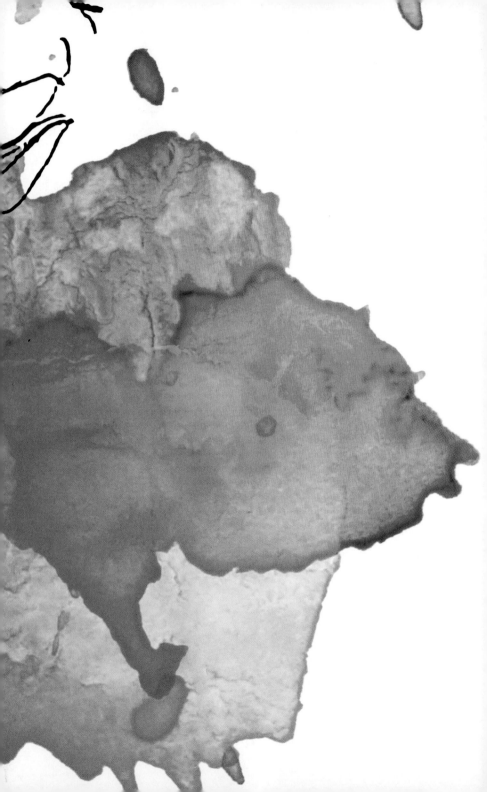

10

For lunch, I grab falafel and a coffee from a street cart and blend in with the rest of the intern crowd. By now I've been in New York long enough that I can tell who the other interns are by the way they're running around, eyes on lists, garment bags in their hands.

Like planned, I hit Mood first. A good portion of the list is findings — clasps, hoops, and fasteners. It makes me wonder what kinds of designs Laura has in mind. She didn't mention anything specific, so it's a bit of a mystery.

When I'm done gathering these, I track down a sales associate and ask her for swatches of fabric. We walk from one aisle to another, getting a mix of colors and textures. My favorites are the bold, beautiful blues and bright, cheerful yellows. I try to envision what Laura might have planned for the different fabrics.

An abstract ikat print in gold and white catches my eye, and I immediately envision it as the basis for a cool, modern ball gown. I'm picturing something floor-length with a full skirt and a strapless bodice. A cinched waist would help provide definition and tone down the volume of the skirt. And beaded floral appliques could add visual interest across the top of the bodice. I make a mental note to work on sketching some ideas when I get back to my dorm room.

"What are you working on?" the saleswoman asks, interrupting my design daydream. She grabs another basket to hold more fabric.

"Um, I'm actually not entirely sure," I admit. "I'm an intern. I'm just picking up stuff for my boss."

"Oh, who are you interning for?" she asks.

"Stefan Meyers," I reply. "I'm with Laura Carmichael now."

The woman's eyes immediately light up. "Laura's a doll! Wait here."

Before I can say anything, the sales associate disappears into the storage room. I rest the baskets on the floor and skim the list again, checking off all the things I've managed to collect so far.

I notice that some of the items on Laura's list have little stars and the word *Fabriqué* beside them. Laura didn't say anything, but I'm guessing that means she wants me to shop there. I've never been to that store, but I've heard enough about it from my suitemates to know it's supposed to be the go-to place for metallic fabrics and out-of-the-box designs.

Looking at the list, I sigh. I've been at Mood for two hours, and I'm only a quarter of the way through the list. My shoulders slump. I should have realized such a long list would take time.

The sales associate finally makes her way back, and my eyes bug out when I see her. She's carrying an enormous pile of material, findings, and embellishments. "I know what Laura likes, and I've been putting stuff away for her," she explains. "Tell her Bree says hi."

"Sure," I say cheerfully. But privately I'm wondering how the heck I'm going to lug all this stuff back.

A few minutes later, I swing the bag Bree gave me over my shoulder. Not only does she have an eye for fabric, she's also an expert packer, consolidating everything in a way that doesn't kill my back.

Fabriqué is next, and as soon as I walk in, I'm greeted by a guy with blue hair. "Enter our mystical world," he says.

EMBELLISHED
IDEA
Sketches

silk jersey dress w/ raw silk pleated skirt

Gold Studded embellished top

→ Gold satin Trousers

IKAT PRINTED KNIT TOP

Gold IKAT SILK Taffeta

Crepe pleated skirt

Laura's List
Mood and Fabriqué
Embellishments

Rib Knit dress →

- Clasps
- Fasteners
- Chains
- Fabrics
- Zippers

Pleated drop skirt

Scattered beading on silk

EMBELLISHED DRESS *Design*

BEADED FLOWER APPLIQUÉS

STRAPLESS BODICE

CINCHED WAIST

GOLD & WHITE IKAT PRINT

FLOOR LENGTH

FULL SKIRT

The way he says it, I almost expect to see crystal balls and a fog machine, but neither appear. The store does have a disco ball, though, which casts funky lights and shadows on the walls. There are no pure cottons here — the rows are filled with metallics, velvets, and spandex, with silks and satins thrown in. Even their findings and embellishments are unique.

I pick up a crystal chain that would make a pretty border. It's not on Laura's list, but I think she'll like it, so I decide to hold onto it. Then I scan the racks and shelves for the fluorescent, gold, and silver fabrics she listed. She didn't write what each piece was for, but I envision them adorning a zipper or accenting a dark color. Or maybe Stefan is thinking of shaking up the spring line with metallic clothing.

"Finding everything you need?" the blue-haired boy asks.

"Yep, but I wouldn't mind coming back here." This store is my new favorite.

I check the list again as I head outside. I'm more than halfway done now, and it's almost five o'clock. Finishing will probably take me another two or three hours, but that was my plan.

I text Laura an update and keep going.

* * *

It's eight o'clock when I finally show up in Laura's office. My legs ache from all the walking, and I'm grateful I wore flats today.

"How did it go?" Laura asks.

"I finished the whole list," I say proudly, setting the pile of bags on the floor.

Laura's eyebrows shoot up in surprise. "No way. Let me see." She goes through all my bags, placing checks beside mine on the list. When she gets to Bree's package, her face lights up. "She's too good to me!"

"She seemed to really like you," I say.

"What's not to like?" says Laura, laughing. "Just kidding. But in this business you need to treat everyone with respect. Some designers don't. They act like everyone has to drop what they're doing and help them immediately. Same goes for interns. If they weren't treated well, they'll do the same to others, like payback. It's a cutthroat business, but there *are* people who will support you. I've worked with a lot of difficult people, but I choose to play nice."

I think of Madison and frown.

"What is it?" asks Laura, taking note of my facial expression.

I don't want to seem like a tattletale, but I have to get it off my chest. Taking a deep breath, I tell her what Madison said.

Laura shakes her head. "I'm not surprised. Like I said, there are all kinds of people. I've noticed that Madison doesn't always seem to have the best attitude, so I wouldn't take it personally."

That makes me feel a little better, but I'm still wondering if Madison was telling the truth. "Do people really feel like she does?" I ask quietly. "Like I shouldn't be here?"

Laura sighs. "I'm sure some people do, but so what? There hasn't been one second when I've felt you don't belong." She pauses and looks at all the packages on the floor. "Wait," she says. "That's why you ran yourself ragged today? To prove something to me?"

I nod, feeling a little silly.

"You don't have to do that, Chloe," Laura says. "I see how hard you've been working. I've even told Stefan. Pace yourself, hon. You have plenty of time to be noticed, plenty of time to shine. You're just starting out in this business."

Until Laura says that, it doesn't hit me that finishing the list was about more than proving myself to the Madisons of the world. A part of me wanted to be a star too. The same part of me that was bummed out when no one introduced me to Stefan at the meeting.

I know Laura's right, I think, *but is it so bad to want to shine now too? Just a little?*

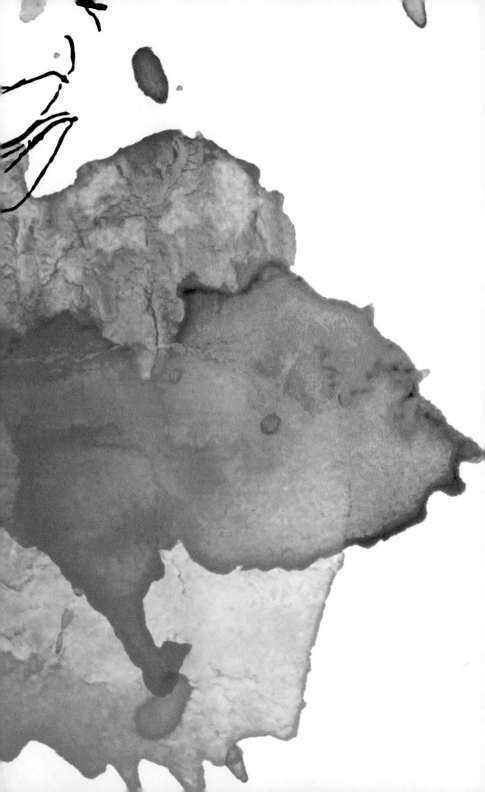

11

The next day, I meet up with Liesel and Jake for lunch. They both give me big hugs as soon as they see me.

"How's the big project with Taylor going?" I ask Liesel.

Her eyes light up. "That project was years in the making. I love collaborating with other designers, but not everyone is open to sharing the spotlight. Taylor is very no-nonsense, and I'm more whimsical. But we're a good balance. She has terrific ideas. I can't wait until the pieces make their debut during Fashion Week."

I think about how long Liesel has been in the business. She said "years in the making." That seems *ages* away. "It would be great if a sample I worked on got the go-ahead," I say. "Especially with Stefan coming tomorrow."

Liesel smiles and shakes her head. "You're just like this one," she says, pointing at Jake. "You two need to remember that it takes time. Designers wait *years* to be noticed. It's wonderful that you're ambitious and a hard worker. But be patient. When you work with other departments, pay attention to what they do."

I remember Bailey mentioning that Stefan moves interns around. Why hasn't Laura said anything about it? *Maybe that means I'll get to stay where I am*, I think hopefully.

"Your work ethic will get you really far," Liesel continues. "I have no doubt you'll have your own line eventually."

I blush. "Thanks."

"I'm not just saying that to make you feel good," Liesel tells me. "I mean it. But, Chloe, you have to have patience, put in your time."

I frown. That's pretty much what Laura said. It makes total sense, but who doesn't want to get noticed sooner rather than later?

"Come on," Jake says to his mom, "what's wrong with going all out? Why shouldn't Chloe be in the spotlight if she has the chance?"

Liesel pats Jake on the shoulder. "Because she doesn't need to be making enemies. She also has lots to learn about the business." She takes a sip of her coffee. "As do you."

Jake rolls his eyes, and I think about what they said. It's funny that Jake and I think alike and Laura and Liesel are on the same page. Who's right?

* * *

Wednesday morning, I'm tacking prototypes onto the bulletin board when Laura runs from her office. "Stefan is coming early!" she says breathlessly. "Help me gather our pockets for the meeting."

Laura and I work quickly, cross-referencing our designs with her notes. Then we pack everything up, including the bulletin board, and lug it to a large conference room. We set up our board and designs beside the others.

Today's meeting is with all the departments, and the room looks like it's been wallpapered with designs. I check out the dress samples and wonder if any of them are part of the line Taylor and Liesel have been working on. Another board has drawings of pantsuits, but they're completely different from Laura's vision, full of pastels. Either Stefan isn't sure what he wants, or the designer didn't ask.

I see Madison sitting beside the other interns. She looks at me, cups her hand over her mouth, and whispers something to the girl beside her. They both laugh, and I turn away.

Stefan walks in, and just like at the first meeting, everyone immediately goes silent. He talks enthusiastically about what's ahead and what he envisions for the new elements of the spring line.

"I see it as splashes of color," he says. Everyone nods like they get it, but I wonder if they really do. "Many designers will be doing pastels. That's what everyone thinks of when they hear spring, right? But not us."

Someone groans, and I wonder if it's the designer with the pastel bulletin board.

"I'm not going to redesign the wheel," Stefan continues. "We will throw in some pastels, but there will be something edgy about them. We will continue expanding the denim line, and I have a vision that will include departments working together. Let's begin."

Stefan goes item by item, pointing out what he likes and doesn't. He doesn't cut anyone down and gives pointers when he can. His critiques remind me of Liesel's. We're there for three hours, and I take notes on all his comments.

Finally Stefan gets to our board and Laura's designs. "This is exactly what I had in mind," he says, smiling wide as he studies Laura's dress. "The scalloped neckline and black trim are a great touch. This will fit perfectly in the spring line. Well done!"

"Thank you, but the idea came from Chloe," says Laura.

With that one comment, I feel every set of eyes in the room focus on me.

"Oh?" says Stefan. "Chloe?"

My face reddens. He doesn't have a clue who I am.

"My intern," says Laura. "The *Teen Design Diva* winner?"

Stefan's eyes find my face, and they light up in recognition. "Tell me more," he says.

"Chloe designed the pocket prototypes," Laura explains. "Her adorable black pocket with the lavender border gave me the idea for this dress."

Laura winks at me, and I'm stunned. I can tell by others' faces that they are too. How many of them would be willing to share their glory like Laura just did?

"Chloe," says Stefan. "You made all these pockets?" He looks at the bulletin board.

"Yes," I say quietly.

"Impressive," he says. "I have to say my two favorites are the one Laura mentioned and the one with the pearl detail. I can definitely work with these for Fashion Week."

"Thank you," I say. I feel like I should say more, but the compliments are more than I could have imagined.

stitched flower

Applique daisies

Painted roses

Satin pipe

Studded + bejeweled

gold stitched? Pattern

Rose appl

crystal studs

crystal studs

Purple trim

trim w/scallop

FINAL POCKET PROTOTYPE Designs

SCALLOPED NECKLINE

POCKET
DRESS
Design

PURPLE DRESS

- Embellishments
- Pockets
- SM Spring line

BLACK TRIM

POCKET PROTOTYPE
LAURA & CHLOE

STRAPPY SANDALS

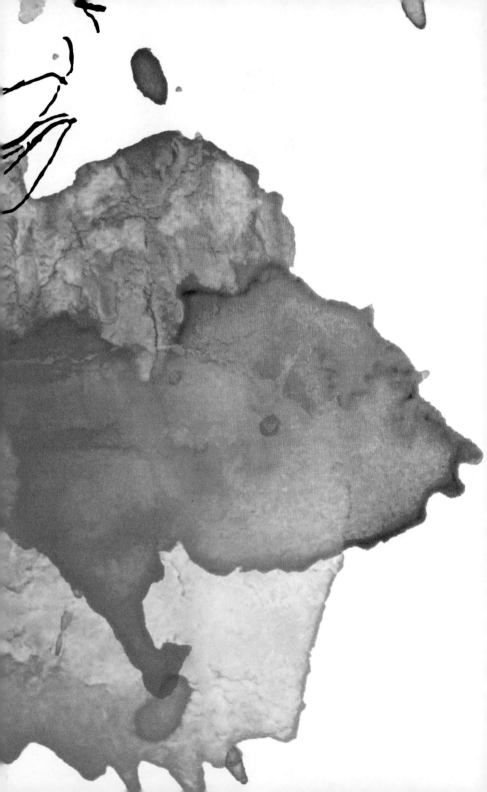

12

"Pizza?" Bailey asks in the dorms that night.

I drop a few dollars in the pile on the floor and take a slice. "Thanks!"

"I heard you guys had a *looong* meeting today," says Avery.

I glance at Madison, but she keeps her eyes on the pizza. "More than three hours!" I say. "Is that normal?"

Bailey laughs. "Girl, I've been to five-hour meetings! But I'll take that over a half-hour meeting that leaves you scratching your head about what to do next."

Avery nods. "Agreed. I had an internship last semester where the meetings were so fast — just in and out. At first I was stoked. But most of the designers needed more direction, so we'd end up doing designs we *thought* the guy wanted and then having to scrap everything when it didn't work. It was a nightmare!"

I think about Stefan's approach. There *are* designs that get chucked, but if you take the time to listen, you at least have a clear direction. "Stefan's not like that," I say. "He's really detailed in the meetings and so supportive."

"I haven't interned there yet," says Avery. "Maybe next summer."

Madison frowns. "Not everyone's time is so wonderful."

Bailey pats her shoulder. "You won't be with Taylor forever. Remember, they switch your department every two weeks."

"Does that always happen?" I say, my stomach turning. I make a mental note to ask Laura tomorrow.

"Don't worry," Madison mumbles, pushing the pizza around on her plate. "I'm sure whoever you're with next will find your designs . . . how did Stefan put it? Oh yeah, 'impressive.'"

Bailey and Avery look from me to Madison. "What's she talking about?" asks Bailey.

I'm not surprised Madison hasn't mentioned Stefan liking my designs. "I had to make pockets for the bulletin board. Stefan liked two."

Avery's mouth drops open. "He knew they were yours?"

I nod. "Yeah, Laura told him."

"Wow," Avery says, raising her eyebrows. "You're really lucky. Most designers wouldn't have given you credit."

"And the fact that Stefan made a point to talk about them at the meeting shows he really liked them," Bailey adds. "He doesn't say things just to be nice."

I blush. "Well, I made loads of pockets. He only said he liked two." It's clearly a big deal that he liked *any*, but if I'm being honest, it did bother me a little that he didn't say much about the others.

Bailey laughs. "We always want more, don't we? Trust us. It's a huge deal. Head designers are thrilled when a design gets added to a line."

I perk up. "He did say something about being able to work with them for his Fashion Week designs."

"That's incredible!" says Avery. "I bet you'll be helping with more than pockets soon enough." She takes my share of pizza money from the middle of the floor and gives it back to me. "Our treat as a congratulations."

I look at Madison and see her scowling at the floor. I feel bad for her even though she hasn't been nice to me. We all want to be noticed. "Maybe when you work with another designer, you'll have a better experience," I say softly.

"Whatever," she snaps. "I need air."

Madison leaves the room, and Bailey shakes her head. "Forget her. Let's celebrate. To Chloe!" she says, raising her pizza slice in the air.

"To Chloe!" echoes Avery.

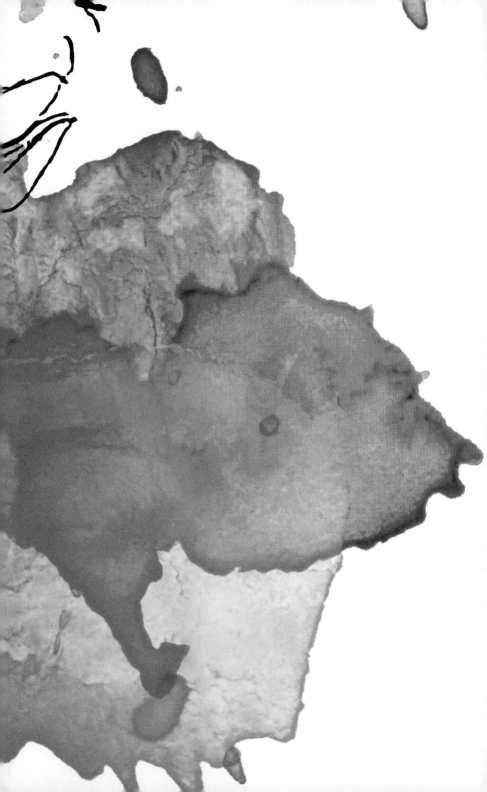

The next morning, I'm still feeling giddy from my pocket triumph the day before. I get to Starbucks extra early, park myself on the leather couch, and take out my sketchpad. This time I focus on a woman at the front of the store. She's leaning against a chair and checking out something on her phone.

I sketch a loose, pale pink A-line dress and chic bob. She's the epitome of a confident, successful New York businesswoman.

I start sketching, taking care to make sure her confidence comes through in my drawing. I love how she's accented her outfit with a leopard-print bag and a multilayered gold statement necklace.

The woman looks up from her phone and catches me looking at her. I start putting away my sketchpad, worried she's going to get annoyed about me drawing her. But she just smiles.

* * *

"There you are, Chloe!" Laura exclaims as I walk into her office later that morning. "I've been waiting for you."

I glance at my watch, worried I might have lost track of time. "Was I supposed to be here earlier this morning?" I ask.

Laura shakes her head. "No, sorry. I'm just excited. I have some good news for you!"

I scan her desk to see if there's a list waiting, but all I see are Laura's sketches. "What is it?" I ask.

"You get a break this morning," Laura tells me. "Take advantage of it, because it happens hardly ever."

That is good news. Sketching at Starbucks this morning was so great. It would be awesome to do some more people watching. But . . . "Why?" I ask her.

Laura cocks her head at me and grins. "This is why I like you. Someone else might have just been happy with the time off. I can tell you always have designing on the brain. You remind me of me."

"What a great compliment!" I say.

"I'm glad you think so." Laura takes a sip of her latte. "About the break. Stefan is really excited about the designs he saw at yesterday's meeting, especially ours —"

"That was so nice of you to give me credit like that!" I interrupt.

"Stefan thought so too," Laura replies, grinning at me. "He was impressed at how well we work together. In fact, it tipped the scales in my favor for a big Fashion Week design he was considering!"

"That's amazing! What is it?" I ask.

"Stefan is still working out the details and will be here this afternoon to discuss, but it's a multi-department project. He wants to do a last-minute addition to Fashion Week that will involve an art deco line and is counting on my department to collaborate with Taylor's," Laura explains excitedly.

I love art deco! It's so glamorous. I can already imagine silk dresses covered with intricate beading. This must be what Liesel has been working on too. She has a great eye for these types of designs. I'm so excited about the new project — until I remember what Bailey said last night about switching departments.

"That's so exciting," I say. "But . . . will I get to help? I heard I might have to start working with someone else next week."

ART DECO
FASHION
Sketches

LONG OR
SHORT?

Evening Designs

BEADED
FRINGE

Laura sighs. "That's the hard part. Honestly, I've been avoiding that discussion because I was hoping Stefan would let me keep you."

My face falls. Just when things sound exciting, I'll have to move.

"Chin up," Laura says with a grin. "I convinced him to let me share you so you can be fully involved in the art deco design."

I'm not sure what this means, but I'm glad I'll still be working with Laura.

"Madison will be moved to sales, and you'll work with me and Taylor," Laura explains. "It will take some adjusting, but I have faith in you. I think you'll be able to handle it."

Laura looks at me expectantly, and my heart flutters with nerves and excitement. This will be a big Fashion Week focus. I was plenty busy with Laura — will adding Taylor be too much?

I take a deep breath. I'm nervous, but if Laura has faith in me, I should too. "I can do it," I say with a big smile. "Thanks so much for the opportunity!"

"Excellent," Laura says. "Take the morning off to relax. Get breakfast, work on your own stuff, whatever you want. I bet you haven't had any time to do your own designs since you've been here."

I nod. "I miss that." I immediately feel guilty for saying so. After all, Laura just told me I'd get to be part of an amazing project.

Laura only smiles. "One day, Chloe Montgomery, you'll have your own intern, and stores will be filled with the CM label."

I head to the elevator, thinking about what Laura and Liesel have both told me recently. It takes patience and experience to succeed in the fashion world. Patience isn't my strong suit, but I'm doing my best.

I find a bench outside and take a seat. Sketchpad in hand and ideas bouncing around in my head, I'm ready. I start to draw, mentally counting down the hours until Stefan's arrival.

"Hey!" someone suddenly yells. I glance up to see a skater dude with spiky hair. He has his eyebrow pierced and is wearing baggy shorts. I watch him do his tricks and pencil in the chain belt holding his shorts up.

"Hey!" he yells again. I look around and don't see anyone there. He does more tricks, and I draw the V-neck collar of his shirt.

Finally the boy stops skating, puts his board under his arm, and walks over. "Hey," he says when he gets close. He'd been calling me all along.

"Um, hi," I say.

"Were you just drawing me?" he asks.

I bite my lip. I know people are weird about that sort of thing. They get self-conscious and don't like to be subjects in someone's notebook. I really need to learn to be more discrete.

"Yeah," I finally say. "I'm sorry. See, I'm a —"

"I know who you are," he says. He puts his hands in his pockets and blushes. "I, um, saw the show."

Now it's my turn to blush. "Oh, wow!" I relax since it doesn't seem like he's mad.

"Yeah, so, uh, can I have that drawing?" the guy asks. "And will you sign it for me?"

My eyes bug out. "You want *this*?" I say. "But it's just a pencil sketch."

"Yeah, but it's a Chloe Montgomery original," he says, acting like that means something important.

I'm speechless but sign my name and give him the drawing.

He holds it carefully, making sure not to wrinkle it. "You have a rubber band?"

"Um, sure." I dig one out of my purse and hand it to him.

He rolls up the drawing. "Thanks!" he says, still blushing. Then he skates away, drawing tucked safely into his backpack.

I stare after the skateboarder, hoping my mouth isn't hanging open. That was surreal. I never would have imagined my design would mean so much to someone. Is it possible that one day, my name will mean something too?

Dear Diary,

I can't believe two weeks of my Stefan Meyers internship have already passed! I still have six weeks to go, but if it's anything like the past couple weeks, it's going to fly by. There's always something new to learn, especially since I'll be changing departments soon. I can't say I'm thrilled about it — working with Laura in knits and denims has been amazing! But apparently it's something Stefan does so interns can get experience in more than one area. And I don't want to complain, so . . . tomorrow I start in dresses with Taylor.

But there is some good news! I'll get to keep working with Laura! She needs help with a last-minute addition to the line Stefan is showing at Fashion Week — a small art deco collection. The tricky (and stressful!) part is going to be splitting my time between two departments — I'll be with Taylor on Monday, Tuesday, Wednesday and with Laura on Thursday and Friday. I've heard rumors (mainly from Madison) that Taylor can be hardcore. I'm a little anxious about having to prove myself again.

Speaking of Madison . . . she's still not my biggest fan. I don't really know why. She's had it out for me since we met. She's convinced I only got this internship because I was on *Teen Design Diva*. Yes, the internship was the grand prize, but I'm also a good designer. She acts like all my successes are a fluke. You'd think she'd be psyched about everyone changing departments so she doesn't have to work for Taylor anymore, but you'd be wrong. As soon as she heard I was looking forward to working with Taylor, she stalked out of our suite. I guess she didn't want me working in that department either.

Thankfully Bailey and Avery have both been really supportive, and staying in the dorms at FIT has been completely surreal. Living here now gives me a taste of what it could be like if I were a student. I wish my mom or Alex were here so I could vent about the Madison stuff. I talk or text with them every day, but I haven't wanted to share any of the downsides of this internship. No need to worry anyone back home. I'll figure the Madison stuff out on my own.

The truth is, it seems like Madison will only be happy if I fall flat on my face. But, newsflash: I've waited too long for this opportunity to let that happen.

Xoxo — Chloe

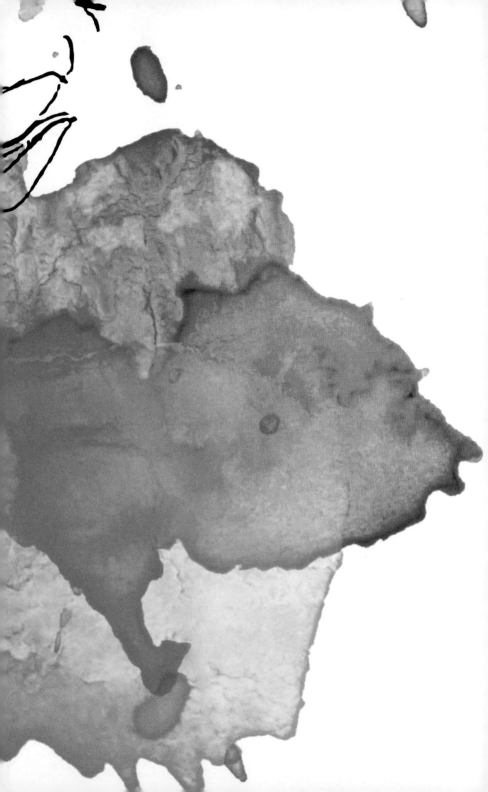

Monday morning, the skies rumble and lightning flashes as I try to keep my umbrella steady. The walk from my dorm at FIT to the subway is a short one, but the wind kicks up, and in seconds, my hair gets drenched. Great. Now I look like a cat that got sprayed with a hose. What a way to begin my first day in my new department. I take a seat on the train, which thankfully isn't too crowded yet, and pull my raincoat tighter around me. At least my outfit is still dry!

I take out my sketchpad, which never fails to calm me, and glance around the subway car, hoping to see something inspiring. Unfortunately, thanks to the rain, everyone is wearing some sort of jacket. Their features are hidden by hoods or wet hair that's plastered to their faces. I focus on a woman wearing an oversized hooded rain cape in a bright, neon yellow. The fabric appears to be lightweight and water-resistant, making it the perfect garment for today's warm but crummy weather. The cape could look shapeless, but the woman has paired it with tight pants and tall boots for a chic, wearable — and more importantly, *dry* — look.

The train lurches to a stop, and the woman grabs the pole beside her. I shade in the color on her raincoat and notice her free hand close around a brightly colored umbrella. The train stops again, and the woman makes her way out the doors. I pack up my sketchpad since my stop is next.

When I reach my stop, I'm calmer — and thankfully somewhat drier — than when I rushed on. I head up the stairs to get out of the gloomy underground, and notice the rain has stopped. Stefan Meyers, here I come.

* * *

According to the information I got from Stefan last week, I'm supposed to report to the fifth floor today. As the elevator takes me there, I check my hair and makeup in the mirrored panels. My hair is no longer dripping,

but it's definitely on the frizzy side. Nothing a few finger scrunches can't fix.

Turning around, I check out my striped knit sweater dress and smooth out a few wrinkles with my hand. I always prefer my own designs, but there was no time to make anything new for this internship. This dress, which I bought from my favorite Santa Cruz store, Mimi's Thrifty Threads, is as close to wearing my own stuff as I'll get. I've paired it with some low-heeled ankle booties, which have miraculously kept my feet somewhat dry.

The elevators whoosh open, and I step out. No one is there to greet me, and I take a moment to check out my surroundings. Even though the workday just started, everyone is clearly busy. Designers are sketching, pinning ideas on inspiration boards, and checking fabric against mannequins. Others are huddled in the corner chatting and sipping coffee, but their eyes are glued to the clock on the wall.

Unlike my first day with Laura, no one stops to stare at me. After two weeks here, I'm old news, and I like it that way. I was getting tired of whispers about "Diva Girl." That's a name Madison started, meant to be an insult. Like people only cared about me because I was on television.

I walk through the aisles, and my face lights up. There are images for art deco inspiration everywhere. From mood boards, to sketches, to books — all showcasing different designs. I stop and look at the beading and fabrics displayed on a nearby mood board, imagining what the glitzy and glamorous styles will look like when they're finished.

"It gives you chills, doesn't it?" a woman's voice says from beside me. I jump, and she chuckles. "Sorry, I didn't mean to scare you. I'm Taylor."

Taylor extends her hand, and I shake it. She has a firm grip, and I immediately understand why Madison was intimidated by her. Even though she's smiling, her severe bun and perfect posture let me know she's all business.

"Chloe," I say.

Taylor nods. "I've heard great things about you from both Laura and Stefan. I hope you won't disappoint me."

I'm about to laugh but stifle the impulse when I realize she's not kidding. "I promise I won't. I'm a hard worker."

"Then we'll get along just fine," Taylor says. "Follow me to your desk, and I'll show you what you'll be doing today."

My desk, an exact replica of the one I had in knits, is located right in front of Taylor's office. *At least I won't have to venture far if I need her help*, I think.

I scan my new workspace. Sitting on top is an overstuffed binder, and on the floor next to it are several bins of fabric. Then I see what's on my seat — a laptop!

"It's here!" I exclaim.

Taylor looks confused for a moment, then notices the laptop. "Oh, right. They delivered it this morning. We still do the majority of our work by hand, but it's nice to have it for note taking or perfecting designs."

"So what am I doing today?" I ask eagerly.

"Today is about me getting to know how you think," says Taylor. "When I work with interns, I like to see their thought process and what they know. It allows me to see just how much direction and guidance you need."

I swallow. This sounds like a test.

"Let's look at these bins," Taylor continues. "Each one is sorted by material. The silks are here, the satins here, tulle in that one, and so forth. Now, let's explore the binder."

Taylor flips it open to the first page. On one half, I see swatches of material — scraps in all different colors and textures. On the other half is a sketch of an outfit with the swatches representing the clothing. The first page has a sketch of a ball gown. The top half is covered with black silk swatches, while the bottom is covered with sheer organza.

"It looks like an inspiration board," I say. "You get a rough image of the outfit before you make the prototype, like a mini-version of a design."

"Exactly," Taylor says, nodding. "I like inspiration boards, but I also like binders. They help me stay organized.

I'd like you to go through the binder, and make a note of your favorite designs. Explain why you do or don't like something. Don't worry about hurting my feelings. Many of these were just brainstorms and never used. Others were from seasons past."

Taylor flips to the back of the binder. "I haven't gotten around to matching these sketches with fabric yet. When you get to this section, I'd like you to try your hand at that. Just like you saw on the other pages. Make sense?"

I nod. "So for those sketches in the back, you want me to go through the bins and choose the fabrics I think would look best on them?"

"You got it," says Taylor.

"But what if it's totally different from what you had in mind?" I ask nervously.

"That's fine," says Taylor. "Like I said, I just want to see how you think. It might seem silly, but it helps me going forward. When you match the fabrics, please do it in your sketchpad, not in the binder. I want to save that for the finished product. I really don't like leaving anything to chance."

Taylor goes back into her office and closes the door. I start poring through the designs, immersing myself in all the details. I know there's no right or wrong, but I *really* hope we're on the same page.

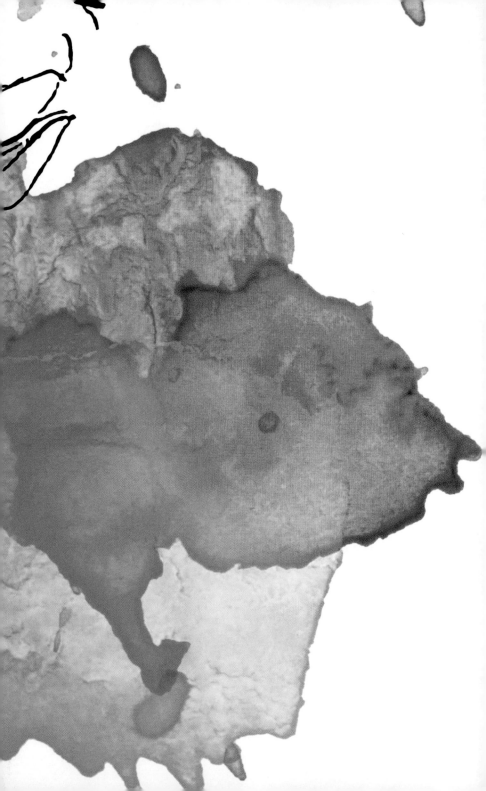

I spend the rest of the morning working, taking my time with each page. Since this is my first full day with Taylor — and my first impression — I want to make sure it's a good one.

I flip a page, and a dress in blinding yellow catches my eye, and I make a note on my "dislike" list. I like the cut of the dress, and I love a pop of color, but this bright neon is not my thing. I'd rather see a solid, neutral dress, maybe in black or khaki, with a neon belt or subtle pattern as an accent. I make a note of that too.

Another page is a mid-length dress with a contrasting belt. I make a note about how the contrast in color brings the outfit to life. Some designs leave me lukewarm. They have all the things I like, such as pops of color and smooth fabric, but something does not work for me. A beige dress with white polka dots and a white belt looks chic, but I'm not totally in love with it. It's a little preppier than my normal style.

I'm excited when I get to the back of the binder. The sketches Taylor created are of flowing dresses with geometric patterns. They definitely look like the preliminary drawings for the art deco line. I pick out a gray silk and pair it with silver threading, then paste the combo into my sketchpad. For another dress, I match a satin top with an organza bottom. Too bad none of the bins have embellishments. Threaded pearls would look pretty.

A few hours later, I take a break for lunch. I run out quickly and buy a sandwich to eat at my desk in the hopes that Taylor will come back early. I can't wait to hear what she has to say about what I've done so far. As I eat, I study the piles of sketches, notes, and designs I worked on this morning. I'm really proud of them, but I can't help but be a little nervous. *What if Taylor hates all the styles I love?* I worry silently.

Finally, Taylor emerges from her office and walks over to my desk. "Let's see what you have," she says.

I watch her face as she flips through my sketches and looks over the notes I made on the laptop. Sometimes she smiles and nods. Other times, her face is unreadable. I take a sip of my water and try to calm my fidgety legs.

After what seems like forever, Taylor says, "For the most part, you and I are on the same page. That is such a relief."

I laugh. "For me too!"

"I'm glad that you're not a fan of the loud, busy prints," she says, pointing to the bright, neon-yellow dress. "These, on the other hand," she says, setting aside my art deco drawings, along with the sample fabrics and designs I've chosen from the bins, "are exactly my style."

I shift my chair closer. "I loved the rich feel of the fabric here," I say, picking up a shimmery silver swatch. I hold it against a sketch of a mermaid-style dress. "This will look great."

Taylor cocks her head. "It's what Stefan had in mind too. He was right on the money putting you here."

I beam. My earlier anxiety is gone, and now I'm filled with excitement.

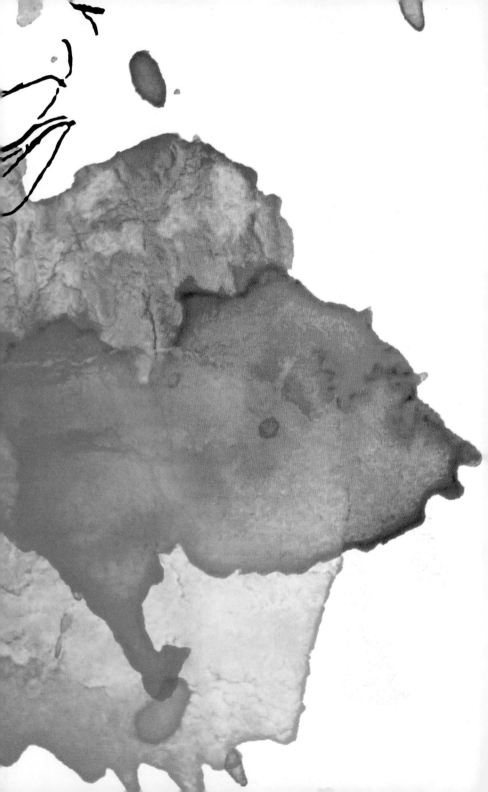

Tuesday morning, coffee in hand, I'm back in the office. It's only seven-thirty, but I was itching to start my day. At eight o'clock on the dot, the elevator doors open, and Taylor makes her way down the hallway. Her arms are loaded with bags, but she manages to balance her coffee cup too. I marvel at how put-together she looks.

"You're here early!" she says, passing my desk to drop off her bags. "That's what I like to see."

I'm glad she's pleased, but I also hope she doesn't expect me to be this early every day. After placing her bags in her office, Taylor eases into a chair beside me, coffee in hand.

"As you know, Stefan made a last-minute addition to the designs being showcased at Fashion Week next month. Now that I know we're on basically the same page design-wise, I'd like you to work on coming up with three art deco-inspired design details that can be carried out throughout this collection," she explains.

I think about what she wants. "You mean like the beading?"

Taylor nods. "Exactly. Then, we just need two more elements that can be our signature within these designs. I also have these binders filled with art deco elements to use as inspiration," she says, placing a crate filled with binders beside my desk. "Get creative."

Taylor heads back to her office, and I pick up my pencil and start flipping through the pages. Time to let my imagination run wild.

* * *

When Taylor checks in after lunch, my sketches are detailed and ready. I enhanced the beading design, showing variations of bead size and type. I also added a sketch of beaded fringe.

Taylor inspects each one, somehow managing not to spill the coffee she's holding. If this were Laura, the drawings probably would have been coffee stained by now. This silly detail makes me miss Laura and her chaos. At least I'll get to see her on Thursday. That feels like a long way away, but Stefan said it's better to spend consecutive days in each department so there's less disruption, and I can finish projects I start.

"Very nice," Taylor says. "I especially like this stitching design of overlapping V's. I can see it embroidered in a satin gown."

That's just how I pictured it too. A floor-length dress made of shimmering silver satin. Taylor takes another sip of her coffee and turns a page in my sketchbook.

"This one is probably my favorite," she says, examining a scalloped sequin pattern.

"I really like it too, maybe for the front of the dress," I say. I imagine the pattern shining, this time on silk fabric, as a model struts on the runway.

Taylor nods. "You have a good eye for this. If I were the warm and fuzzy type, I'd probably be hugging you right now."

I grin. "Mental hug?"

Taylor laughs. "Sure. I'm glad you made so much progress on this. We only have one more day together this week, and then I won't see you again until Monday. I'm going to keep you super busy, but I think you can handle it."

I think about how much Madison complained about Taylor, and how nervous that made me. But these two days haven't been bad at all! "Definitely," I say. "I'm up for anything!"

Draped Cowls

Beaded
Deco
Patterns
- Scalloping
- Chevron
- Geometric

DOODLES
AND
Ideas

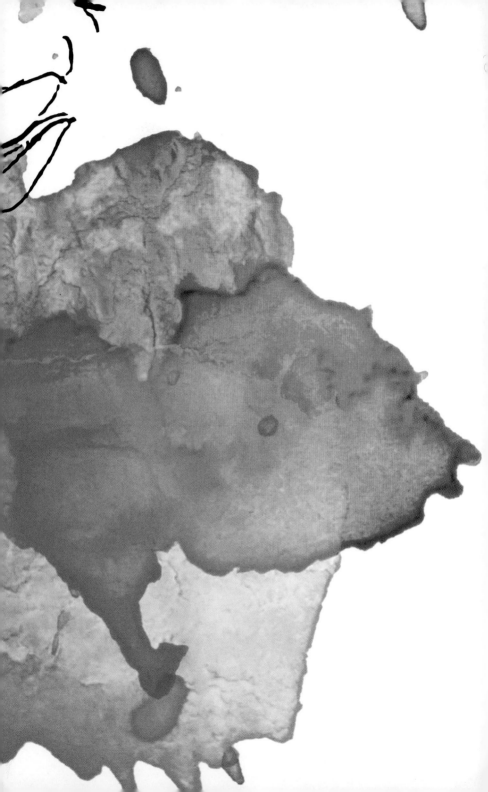

Wednesday morning, I wake up to a text from Taylor telling me to check my e-mail. When I do, my jaw drops. There are more than three pages of items she needs me to pick up for her. She wasn't kidding when she said she was going to keep me busy!

I feel someone peering over my shoulder and have a hunch that it's Madison. Sure enough, I turn around and see her smirking at me.

"No break for you today, huh?" she says. She attempts to sound concerned but totally fails.

I print out the pages and close my laptop. "Better than being bored all day, right?"

Madison shrugs. "I'm just glad I don't have to deal with Princess Taylor anymore."

"We get along fine," I say.

Madison rolls her eyes. "You would," she mumbles.

I decide to just let her comment slide. It's not worth it. Instead, I grab the pages and head out the door, pausing to say goodbye. Instead of answering, Madison pops in her headphones and starts sketching.

* * *

As I head to the subway, I skim Taylor's e-mail again. There's a P.S. at the end telling me to try M&J Trimming. I've never been to that store, so that's something new. I try to push Madison's rude behavior out of my mind and focus on the task ahead of me but give up after a few unsuccessful attempts.

Instead, I whip out my sketchpad and focus on drawing. Madison's head, complete with earbuds, fills my page. I add a lightweight, off-the-shoulder sweater, darkening the lines. Next I sketch a pair of summer-weight shorts. Even drawing Madison, sketching is still therapeutic.

Just as I add espadrilles I think Madison would hate, the train stops at Avenue of the Americas. I make a beeline for the subway doors and search for the Exit sign. It's only

ten o'clock, but my hair is already starting to stick to my neck. It's always hotter underground, but it's especially sweltering today. Thankfully, M&J Trimming is right in front of me.

I remember how tingly I felt when I first walked into Mood, and the feeling is back. What Mood is to fabric, M&J is to embellishments. Never in my life have I seen so many trimmings. Everywhere I look I see more lace, ribbons, studs, and crystals. If I were to dump the contents of the store on the floor, it would be deep enough for a swan dive.

I check Taylor's list and take in every corner and shelf. What I'm seeing is only the beginning. As I learned from my shopping trip for Laura, tracking down everything on the list will probably take hours. Even so, I can't wait to jump in and start shopping.

I'm pulled in many directions, but I try to focus on one item at a time. I start with a wall that says "Crystals," one of the items on Taylor's list, and choose a variety of shapes and sizes. I admire the way light reflects off them before dropping them in my basket. Rhinestones hop into my basket next, then it's on to the bright pink wall labeled "Buttons."

I watch others as I shop. Some people gather their items briskly, while others seem to linger like I do. Studs and pearls beckon, and I toss them into my basket along with embroidered trim in a variety of colors and patterns. Taylor has "chains" on the list, so I grab gold and silver strands, both thin and thick. I imagine them on a dress collar or accenting something off the shoulder.

The hours pass with me going from one aisle to another, switching my basket for a cart when it gets to be too heavy. It's after three o'clock when Taylor texts to check up on me. I check off the final five items and text back that I'm just about done. When I head out the doors, arms loaded with bags, my legs ache. But it's the best ache I've had in a long time.

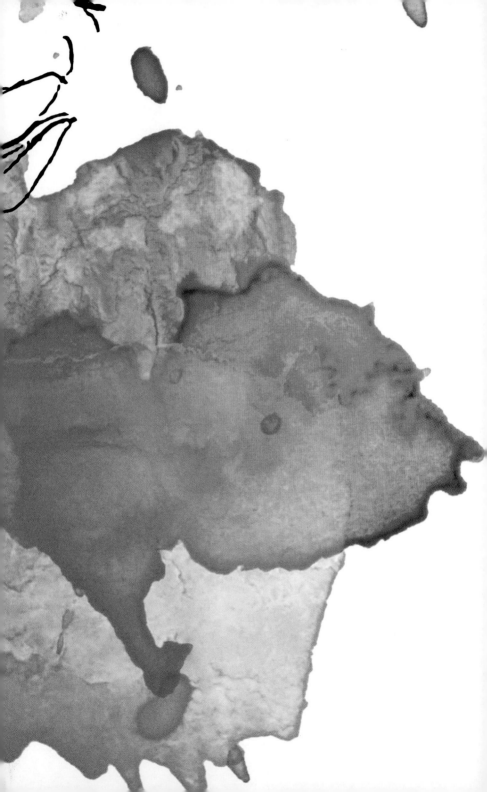

When I arrive at the office on Thursday, my first day back with Laura, I'm feeling super accomplished. Not only did I make it through my first days in a new department, I also managed to impress my new boss. Spending the next two days with Laura will be the perfect end to my week.

I step onto the seventh floor — all giddy and happy — but then I see Laura's office. All the hard work I put into organizing her desk last week is totally invisible. Papers and scraps cover Laura's table, and her coffee cup teeters on the edge.

"Hey," I say, hesitating at the door. "How can I help?"

Laura's head swings in my direction like she's surprised to see me. "Oh, thank goodness you're here!" she says. "This arrangement has not been working for me at all."

I'm flattered, but the dark circles under Laura's eyes make me feel really bad for her.

Laura smiles. "It's my fault. I did too good a job convincing Stefan how competent I am when I had you full-time. Now that you're gone for the first part of each week, it's killer!"

I want to help but have no idea which mess to tackle first. Laura scans the inspiration boards hanging in her office and stops at one with jackets. "Let's start here," she says.

I step forward and study the board. Some of the jackets have sleeves, and some are vests. Some are form fitting, others looser. I look for some kind of theme that screams *Stefan Meyers* but come up short. Just then, the assignment I did for Taylor on my second day pops into my head.

"Are you looking for a way to pull them all together? Some kind of signature design that runs through all the pieces?" I ask.

"Exactly," Laura says. "This is part of the art deco addition Stefan wants to include in Fashion Week. He wants a few ideas that can be interwoven within this jacket line. Does that make sense?"

This is *exactly* what I had to do for Taylor! I totally have this.

"Completely!" I tell her.

LINE DESIGN ON COLLAR

JACKET & VEST Designs

ART DECO STITCHING

SCALLOPED EDGE AT NECK & CUFF

SCALLOPED COLLARS!?

· Vests
Cropped Jackets
· Interesting Collars

Laura looks relieved. "I knew I could count on you. Do you have any questions?"

I smile wide. "Nope. I'm good."

Laura bites her lip and flips through some sketches. "Just to make sure, I'm going to leave you with these boards and drawings. Scan them to get a feel for the jackets. Pay extra attention to the art deco designs. Stefan wants them paired with the dresses you've been working on for Taylor. Use this sketchpad for your finished designs."

I take the boards, sketches, and Laura's sketchpad and carry them to my desk. Laura definitely looks less tense than when I first walked in. I pile the designs around me and start looking through them. There are embroidered collars, embellished sleeves, and intricately stitched lapels. There are so many options, my eyes start to swim.

After a while, each one starts to look the same, and I put them aside. *Laura only gave me these in case I didn't know what I was doing*, I reason. *But I already do. Taylor loved my ideas. They'll be perfect for Laura too.*

I look through my own sketchpad for the rough designs I did for Taylor and rip out the pages so they're easier to copy. I imagine the look of surprise on Laura's face when she sees how quickly I can produce what she wants.

I compare the drawings for Laura with those I did for Taylor. The dresses and jackets will click perfectly. Same beaded design, same fringe. If the pattern worked for Taylor, Laura is bound to love it too.

I glance at all the boards and sketches Laura left for me and feel relieved that I won't have to finish looking through them. Imagine how long that would take! And why bother when I'm able to recreate the same design? *That was some quick thinking*, I tell myself. I copy the patterns, and in an hour, I'm done!

"How's it going?" Laura asks, sticking her head out of her office.

"Done!" I say, beaming.

Laura looks at her watch. "Really? I thought this would take the whole morning." She seems worried.

"Well, I had a clear vision," I say, but it sounds kind of lame and rehearsed. Maybe once Laura sees what I did, she won't be concerned anymore.

"Let's see what you came up with," Laura says. She picks up the drawings I did, and I study her unsmiling face as she flips through them. "You had time to look through the jacket designs?" she asks, motioning to the books and boards she gave me earlier.

A pit forms in my stomach. She doesn't like what I did at all. "I looked through some of them," I say quietly.

Laura sighs and shakes her head. "I'll be right back," she says, walking into her office.

What did I do wrong? Taylor had said I had a "good eye." I scan my drawings again. Maybe I missed an important detail? Nope. They look just like the sketches I did for Taylor.

Laura emerges from her office holding drawings. "These are the designs you did for Taylor, right?" she says, placing the drawings on my desk.

I look through them. "Yes."

"Chloe, I never pegged you as one to take the easy way out. What happened?"

My head is swimming. What is she talking about? Who took the easy way out? "I — I don't understand."

Laura stares at me. Disappointment is all over her face. She has never looked at me that way before. "Why do you think I gave you all those things to look at?"

"To get ideas," I whisper.

Laura nods. "Exactly. If I wanted you to copy what you did for Taylor, why would I do that?"

My eyes tear up. I put the drawings I did for Laura and Taylor side-by-side. They're rip-offs of my own work. I look down at the floor.

"If you were confused, you should have asked what I wanted," Laura tells me. Her voice is soft, but firm. "You should have looked at what I gave you."

"I'm sorry," I say. "I thought that's what you wanted."

Laura looks skeptical. "Really?"

I shrug. I don't know. Maybe I just wanted to get the work done quickly and impress her. But I don't want to say that. How would it look if I admitted to taking the easy way out? Besides, that's not what I did, is it? I was just trying to be efficient. Why waste time looking through dozens of designs if I knew what she wanted?

I feel Laura's eyes on me, but I don't want to lift my head. I dig the toe of my sandal into the carpet.

"Maybe working in two departments is too much for you," Laura finally says. "I really need your help here, but not like this. Why don't you take the rest of the day off? I need to talk to Stefan. I'm not sure this is going to work. Maybe we're better off moving you out of my department."

Moving me out of her department? I think, panicked. *Talking to Stefan?* "I said I was sorry!" I say, too loud and snippy. Suddenly, I feel like a kid who's about to throw a tantrum.

Laura puts her hand on my shoulder. "I know. But I need to think about what's best for the department and what's best for Stefan Meyer. I'll see you tomorrow."

Then she walks away.

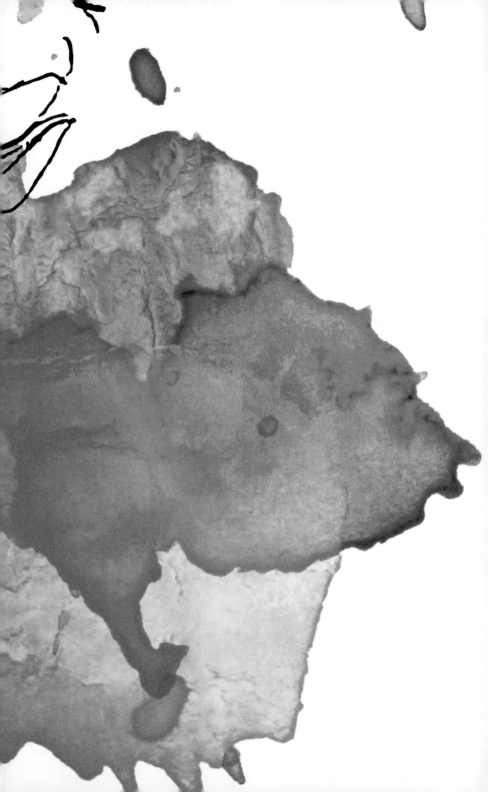

19

I debate going back to my dorm, but I know I'll only replay the last hour over and over in my head. Instead, I decide to hit the pavement. Usually, the city noise makes clearing my head easy, but not today. I really screwed up. And now it might cost me my spot with Laura. I shake my head. I was so desperate to prove I could do everything, and now it seems like I've done the exact opposite.

My stomach grumbles, but I can't bring myself to eat. I wander the streets looking at everyone around me. A woman wearing a printed headscarf and a gold necklace double-wrapped around her neck leans against a building to chat on her cell phone. A breeze rustles her long skirt.

I search for a bench so I can sit and sketch her, but there's none around. I settle for closing my eyes and holding the image for later.

The more I walk, the more I see outfits begging to be drawn. When I spot a cafe with outdoor tables, I order a drink, pull out my pad, and sit down. I focus on a teenage girl waiting for the bus. Her long bangs fall over one eye as she plays with the fringe on her crop top. I use my pencils to outline the top, then add her high-waist shorts. She cranes her neck, and the long, heart-shaped pendant she's wearing around her neck moves with her. She shifts her feet impatiently, and I add flat sandals to my drawing.

The bus finally comes, and the girl disappears. The knot in my stomach has lessened, but I still need to talk to someone. I put my sketchpad away, grab my drink, and let my feet lead me. Soon, I'm standing in front of Liesel McKay's store. She's a former *Design Diva* winner, and we bonded when she was my mentor during my competition.

I step into the store, and the calm I was starting to feel disappears the moment I see Liesel. She takes one look at me and changes the store's sign to CLOSED.

"Spill," she says.

A few minutes later, we're seated near the dressing rooms, and I'm doing just that.

"Laura said she wanted a few design themes that could be integrated with the jackets for Stefan's art deco line. I did the same thing for Taylor, only with dresses. Laura gave me designs to reference, but there were so many. I figured I knew what I was doing and just copied the same designs I did for Taylor," I say, voice breaking. "And now Laura's not sure she wants to keep working with me. She said she needs to talk to Stefan."

Liesel pats my hand. "I know it feels like it, but even if it comes down to that, it's not the end of the world," she says. "You'll still be able to work with Taylor, right?"

"I guess," I mutter.

Liesel smiles. "Then maybe that's the best solution. You'll be able to focus on one department."

"But I don't want to stop working with Laura. Especially like this. I messed up, right?" I ask. I busy myself examining my coffee lid so I don't have to look Liesel in the eyes. I wait for her to tell me Laura overreacted, and that my instincts were spot on. I want her to say I was only being efficient.

Instead, Liesel says, "A little. But we all have. And do. The key is to understand your mistake and learn from it."

I sigh. "I guess I just wanted to come across as an expert, you know? Show everyone I belong? I figured I'd get this assignment done in a flash and impress her."

Liesel nods. "I think you've proved that already. Didn't Laura show her faith in you by praising your pockets in front of Stefan? You shouldn't feel like you need to prove yourself every second."

I look up from my drink. "I just don't like asking questions about everything —"

Liesel cuts me off. "Asking for help or more explanation when you don't understand something is a sign of maturity. It shows that you're conscientious. It's better to ask too many questions and do the project right than to not ask enough and do double the work later."

I nod. I get what Liesel is saying, but . . . what Laura said about me cutting corners still nags at my brain. "Laura thinks I took the easy way out," I say quietly.

Liesel cocks her head. "Did you?"

I shrug. "Maybe? I thought of all the projects Laura had and how I could help her. I figured if I got this done quickly, I could do more for her. Plus, if I asked her if what I was doing was okay, she might say it wasn't, and then the assignment would take forever, and . . ." My voice trails off.

Liesel sighs. "Look, hon. I know you're not one to shirk responsibility. And from what you've said about Laura, she knows you're a hard worker. But ultimately, it's her decision — and Stefan's. It's out of your hands.

Go back to your room. Think up some killer ideas. And no matter what tomorrow brings, you'll start fresh. Deal?"

I nod, my eyes getting teary again.

Liesel hands me a tissue. "None of that. Tomorrow will be a better day." She ducks behind the cash register and rummages through a jewelry box, eventually pulling out an antique-looking gold chain with a sun pendant at the end. "Here," she says, handing it to me. "It's a reminder that things can always get brighter."

"Thank you," I say, putting it on. I give Liesel a hug and head back to my dorm. Time to figure out how to make tomorrow brighter.

PRINTED HEADSCARF

Sun pendant necklace
from Liesel

GOLD
NECKLACE

NYC
WOMAN
Sketch

LONG, FLOWY
SKIRT

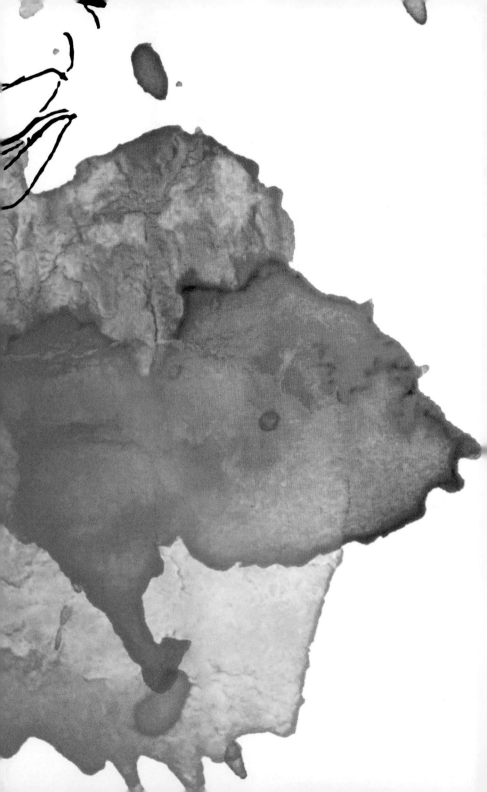

Friday morning, I'm up early. I slip on black shorts, a white lace top, and layers of pearl necklaces, then head to work.

After leaving Liesel's yesterday, I spent the remainder of the day brainstorming and sketching. I tried out one idea after another. Finally, something clicked. I can't wait to share my drawings with Laura. I just hope it's enough to convince her to let me stay.

When I arrive at work at eight o'clock, I walk tentatively into Laura's office. "Hi," I say. "I brought a peace offering." I place a caramel macchiato on her desk.

Laura smiles. "Thanks," she says, taking a sip.

I look down nervously. "About yesterday . . . I'm really sorry. I was wrong. If I had a question, I should have asked. And you were right about me cutting corners . . ." I trail off and rub the beads on my necklace between my fingers, feeling nervous.

Laura nods but doesn't say anything.

"Anyway," I continue, "I'm really sorry. That's all I wanted to say. I hope you'll give me the chance to make it up to you and prove that I deserve to be here."

"Well, everyone makes mistakes," Laura agrees. "I spoke to Stefan, and the fact is, I need the help here. I don't have time to train a new intern, so we both agreed to give you another chance. After all, today is a new day, right?"

I let out a breath and relax. "Right. Which is why I spent yesterday coming up with a plan." I pull my sketchpad out of my bag and open it to my newest designs. I sketched a variety of collar designs that can be used to distinguish the jackets.

Laura looks at my pages. Her smile grows wider with each drawing. "Yes!" she says. "This is perfect. Collars are a great way to differentiate dressy jackets. Not only can we make inspiration boards with the various types of jacket collars, we can also embellish them."

She takes a book of designs from her desk and hands it to me. "Here are some collars Stefan wants to use. See how you can incorporate them in your designs," she says. "Remember the detailed designs you did for the pockets?"

I nod. How could I forget? I've been living off Stefan's compliments on my pockets since that meeting.

"I want designs that detailed for the collars," Laura continues. "After you and I talk about them, I'll have you create prototypes for them. Remember, those are mini-versions of a design? Big enough to fit onto the boards. Then, Taylor and I will discuss how to incorporate them into the line to complement her dresses. Sound good?"

"Got it," I say. This time, there will be no cutting corners.

At my desk, I pore over the pages of Stefan's designs. Then, I work on sketching a variety of collars. I envision dresses printed with signature art deco geometric patterns, accented by solid jackets with cool collars.

I sketch a shawl collar with rounded lapels and think about how different materials can set it apart. Would it look best in silk or velvet? I sketch other samples, including a notched collar, which can give the illusion of a slender silhouette. A fichu lace collar could soften a piece. I add embellishments to the designs as well. Adding pearls or beading on the edges can spice up a jacket.

"I ordered Chinese," Laura says, suddenly appearing beside me.

EMBELLISHED
COLLAR
Designs

Golden Pearls

Topstitching

Peak lapels

embellished w/pearls

Mandarin collar

Scallop shawl collar

Notch collar

I glance up, surprised. I'd been so engrossed in my sketching that I didn't even hear her approach. Nor did I realize it was past lunchtime.

"These are really good," Laura says, leaning over my shoulder to check out my sketches so far. "I love all the variations."

"Thanks," I say proudly.

"Let's go to my office and discuss the prototypes." She pauses and puts her hand on my shoulder. "You're on your way to redeeming yourself."

I beam. I feel good about today's work, but it's even better hearing Laura's compliment.

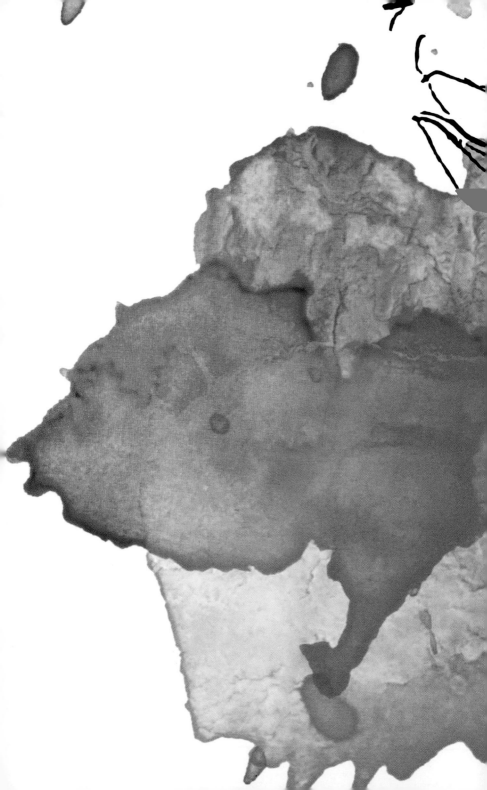

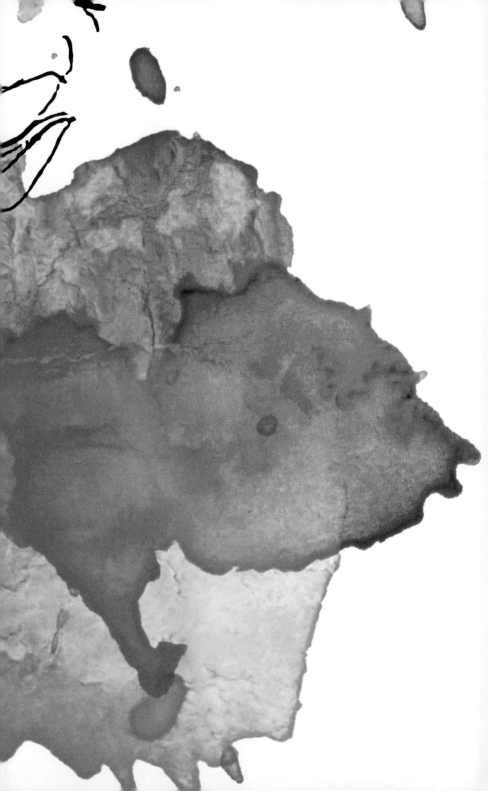

Saturday morning, I wake up to banging. At least it sounds like banging in my half-asleep state. When I open my eyes, the bedroom is empty, but I hear voices coming from the common area. *Why is everyone up so early on a weekend?* I wonder groggily.

I roll over to look at my alarm clock and see that early isn't quite accurate. It's already eleven o'clock! Whoa. I can't remember the last time I slept so late! As I stretch my legs over the side of the bed and debate whether I should join the waking world, someone knocks on the bedroom door.

"You awake, Chloe?" my suitemate Bailey calls.

"Barely," I say, "but you can come in."

Bailey opens the door a crack and squeezes in, closing it behind her. "There's a *cuuuute* boy asking for you," she says, grinning and wiggling her eyebrows. "Says his name is Jake."

My heart skips a beat. I met Jake McKay, Liesel's son, back when I was auditioning for *Teen Design Diva*. And Bailey is right — he is cuuuute. I thought I'd be seeing him a lot more once I started my internship and we were both in New York, but it's been almost two weeks since we hung out at the Ripley's Believe It or Not! museum.

"Great!" I say, my cheeks reddening. "Can you please tell him I'll be out in ten minutes?"

"You got it," Bailey agrees. "But I want to know more about him!"

After Bailey leaves, I slip into a sundress and sandals and check my face in the mirror. Ugh. All those early mornings have made my eyes tired and my skin pale. Thankfully, a layer of moisturizer, a few dabs of concealer, and some bronzer do the trick. Totally ready, and it doesn't look like I just rolled out of bed at all!

"Hey!" says Jake as soon as I step into the common room. Before I can say anything back, he lifts me up and gives me a hug.

Bailey and Avery giggle, and Madison's jaw falls so low it looks like it's going to scrape the floor.

"Hey, yourself," I say, blushing. I love Jake's hugs, but it's a little embarrassing in front of my roommates. "This is a nice surprise."

"Glad you think so," Jake says with a smile. "I figured you've been so busy, I might have a better chance with the element of surprise. Are you free today?"

"Definitely," I agree.

Jake takes my hand and starts to head out. "Nice meeting you all!" he calls back behind him.

"Have fun!" Bailey hollers, giving me a wink.

When we're safely outside the room, Jake says, "Sorry about that. I'm just excited to see you!"

"It's okay. I'm happy to see you too. It's been kind of a rough week," I say.

Jake squeezes my hand as we head into the sunshine. "Yeah, my mom said something like that, but she didn't give me deets."

I fill him in, and when I'm done, Jake looks sympathetic. "Yeah, that's rough," he agrees. "But it sounds like you totally stepped up to the plate and hit it out of the park with yesterday's designs."

I laugh. "Nice baseball metaphors."

We stop at a kiosk and Jake buys us coffee and egg sandwiches. "So, what do you want to do today now that I've managed to steal you away?" he asks.

"Want to go to the Met?" I suggest. "I've been dying to see their dress exhibit. I think it will inspire me."

"Sure," Jake agrees. "But after the dresses, you have to promise we'll hit their sword and armor collections."

I wrinkle my nose, picturing case after case of daggers and knightly gear, but a deal's a deal. "I promise," I say. But privately I think, *But no one said the time spent looking at dresses and armor had to be equal* . . .

* * *

Jake is a good sport as we move from one dress design to another. I've always been into fashion, but the stuff at the Met is totally blowing my mind. We pause at Rudi Gernreich's Kabuki dress. I love the way he combined styles here, blending the kimono with geometric patterns. The belt rests below the bust instead of at the waist, resembling an empire-line dress.

"He's fantastic," I say. "I love that he didn't play it safe. At the time, his ideas were thought to be scandalous. He broke so many barriers."

Jake eyes the dress. "I remember reading about him too. I really respect designers who don't play by the rules." He gives my hand a squeeze. "I bet your designs will be rebellious."

I smile. "I can see it now. Chloe Montgomery ——
Renegade of Style."

Jake grins. "Exactly."

I laugh but secretly I hope that's true. I don't want to be
the one who follows the trends. One day, *I* want to design
the trends others copy.

We view more of Gernreich's work, including the
black wool minidress with half-moons all over it. My eyes
tire looking at the dizzying pattern, but they're refocused
by the red ribbons on the sleeves.

"A style like this might work for Laura's knit line," I
say. Stefan seems like a progressive designer who'd go for
something unique.

We move on to the evening dresses, and I stop beside
a display of art deco-inspired creations. A soft pink dress
with a scalloped, beaded skirt and delicate embroidery
catches my eye. The pattern is a little busier than what
Taylor had in mind, but the scalloped pattern gets my brain
working. It could be gorgeous on a dress she's designing. Or
maybe even a scalloped pattern on a jacket! It's a little out
there, but it could work.

Jake drags behind me, and his eyes glaze over. I could
look at these dresses for hours, but I know he's probably
had his fill.

I link my arm through his. "Swords?" I ask.

His eyes light up. "You're sure you're done?" he asks politely.

"Not really," I tease. I feel bad when his face immediately falls. "Just kidding," I add quickly.

Jake's smile takes over his entire face, and he practically skips to the sword exhibit. I take one last look at the designs around me. After this outing, I'll have even more ideas for Taylor come Monday morning.

RUDI GERNREICH *Fashions*

MOD DESIGNS

RED ACCENTS

SLEEVELESS GRAY DRESS

- Dress Exhibit
- Sword Exhibit
- Ideas for Taylor

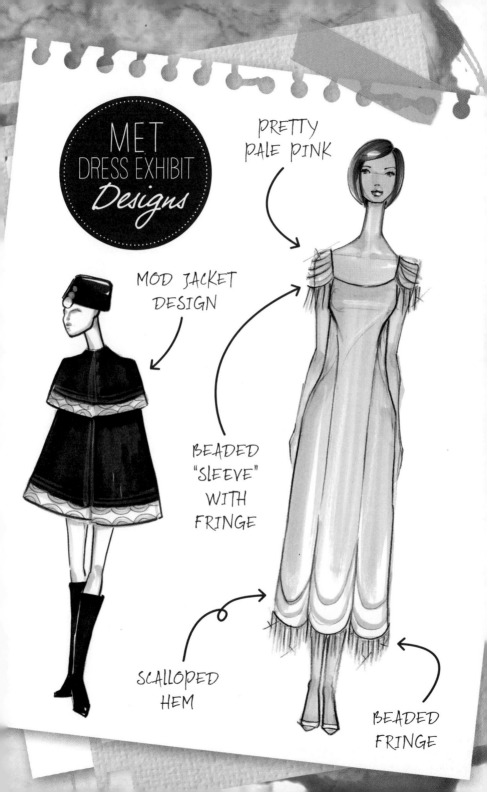

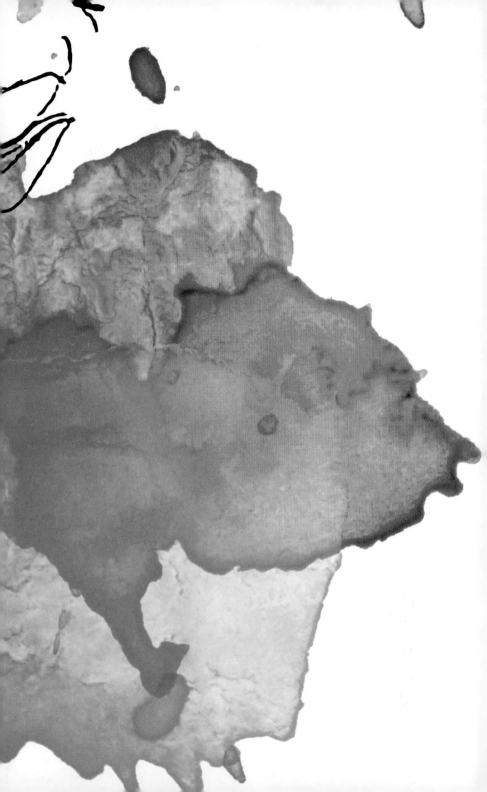

22

On Monday, I wake up raring to go. Saturday put me in a fab mood. Not only did I get to see Jake, but there's something to be said about strolling around New York at my own pace. No errands or missions — just me enjoying what the city has to offer.

I hear Bailey, Avery, and Madison in the common room and head out to join them for breakfast. I've been trying so hard to make a good impression at work that I've been getting there early every day. Usually my suitemates are still sleeping when I leave, so this is a change.

"Pull up a chair," Avery says when I emerge from my room. I take a seat, and she hands me a bowl.

"I should take a picture of this momentous occasion," Bailey jokes. "I think this is the first time all four of us have been on the same morning schedule."

"Join the fun," says Madison, passing me the cereal box and milk. She manages to do it without looking at me, but at least she's acknowledging me.

Bailey and Avery exchange secret smiles, then look at me expectantly. I know they're dying to hear about Jake, but I don't know if I want to go there yet. Especially with Madison. I wish my best friend, Alex, was here. Texting with her is so not the same as real, one-on-one girl talk.

"OMG," Bailey finally says, "I'm going to have to pull it out of you, aren't I?"

I eat a spoonful of cereal and pretend I don't know what she's talking about. "What do you mean?" I ask innocently.

Avery laughs and rolls her eyes. "The boy from the other day — Jake. How long have you been together? What's his story?"

I stall. Together? Jake and I have been hanging out, but is he my boyfriend? We have fun when we get together, but what will happen when I go back to California in September and he's on the other side of the country in New York City? Ugh. So many things I didn't even stop to think about.

"Um," I begin, "he's great! I like his mom too. Liesel McKay?"

Madison breaks her icy facade and stares at me. "Liesel McKay? No way! I love her stuff! Did she, like, introduce you guys when she mentored you on *Teen Design Diva*?"

"No. We actually met at an art fair back in California," I explain. "I had no idea who his mom was at the time. When I found out, I almost died."

Bailey and Avery laugh. "I bet!" says Bailey.

Madison taps her purple fingernails on the table. "And then she just *happened* to be your mentor? I'm sure *that* wasn't rigged at all." She snorts.

I sigh. Re-enter the same old Madison. I knew that nice moment was too good to be true. "Well, on that note, I should probably get going," I say. "See you guys later."

"Don't go!" pleads Avery. "We didn't finish hearing about your boy!"

"Another time," I promise. "I'm sure Taylor has a list of things for me today. The sooner I get started, the better."

As I walk out the door, I hear Avery say, "Madison, why do you have to be so mean?"

"I'm just saying it like it is," says Madison. "It's not my fault Chloe is too sensitive."

Bailey starts to reply, but I close the door. I'm starting to get used to Madison's digs. She reminds me a lot of my back-home rival, Nina LeFleur. And like my mom has told me before, there's always going to be a Nina somewhere.

What nags at me more is Avery's "your boy" comment. Jake isn't mine. And while an hour ago I was happy just hanging with him when we could, now I'm wondering if I want more.

* * *

It's not even nine o'clock when I step off the elevators onto the fifth floor, but Taylor is already lurking by my desk. When she sees me, she glances at her watch, then at the clock on the wall, and frowns.

"I was hoping I'd see you earlier today since it's been days, but what can you do, right?" Taylor says.

I take a deep breath. This must be the side of Taylor that Madison got to see a lot. There's no point in saying I'm not supposed to start until nine or that I came in extra early and stayed late last week. I can tell Taylor doesn't want to hear any of that.

Instead, I plaster on a smile. "I'm eager to get started. What's on the agenda today?"

"Well, uh," Taylor says, clearly taken aback by my no-arguing stance. "I have some gorgeous sketches, and I'd like you to make prototypes of them. They have your embellishment and beading ideas incorporated, and I want to see how they look." She puts a portfolio of sketches on my desk and walks back to her office. "I'll check on you in a few hours." With that, the door starts to close.

I quickly look around and realize that I don't see fabric, thread, or the boards Taylor wants me to pin things to. "Wait!"

"Yes?" Taylor says in a clipped, frosty tone. She's clearly not happy, but I'm not making the same mistake I made with Laura. I'm doing everything right the first time.

"How should I make the prototypes, and where are the boards?" I ask, keeping my voice cordial.

"What do you mean, where —" Taylor stops and looks around, then mutters something under her breath before marching into her office. She's back almost immediately, wheeling a cart with boards and materials.

"Sorry," Taylor says, still sounding a bit irritated. "Sometimes people don't leave things where they're supposed to. Oh, and I forgot to mention, but we had a lot of fabric scraps lying around, so for these prototypes you'll get to work with the real thing. Enjoy."

Nice! I glance at the cart to make sure it has everything I need. "Thanks," I say, but Taylor has already disappeared into her office and closed the door.

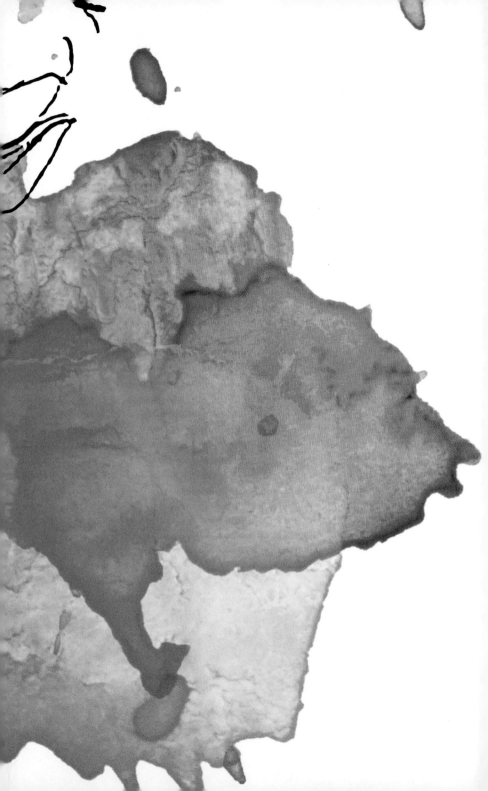

With Taylor and her attitude gone, I dive into the sketches and photos. It takes more than an hour to sort through everything, but I take my time and make notes. Then, I search through the bins and drawers on the cart, pulling out beads, bits of fabric, a needle, and thread.

I've sewn my own clothes for years using a machine, and thanks to *Teen Design Diva*, where we often had to hand sew, I've become even more of an expert at putting things together. At least for prototypes, the stitching doesn't have to be elegant or precise. It's more important to see how the fabric and designs go together. By looking at the prototypes, designers can get a feel for what the garment is supposed to look like. Sometimes, colors or fabrics seem like they'll be a good fit, but it's not until you see them actually sewn together that you get a real understanding of how the design will look.

I take out a silk charmeuse fabric in beige and cut a square neckline, then stitch something resembling cap sleeves. For the final touch, I decide to give Taylor options. I sort the beads in front of me. In one prototype, I sew beading to cover the bust area. In another, I make the entire gown fully beaded.

The next sketch is of a gown in silver chiffon. I pull the fabric from a drawer and lay it on my desk. I rub the soft cloth between my fingers. Wearing this fabric is practically guaranteed to make anyone feel beautiful. I check the sketch and pin back pieces to create a plunging neckline with thin shoulder straps and an open back. Then I outline the fabric for the bias cut and empire waist. The crystal embroidery, perfect for an art deco garment, makes the material shimmer and pulls the design together. I touch the delicate beading and imagine the dress on the runway. If only I could model it.

I work on more pieces as time passes and am grateful Taylor hasn't checked in. Being left alone with the fabric is peaceful. It's fascinating to me that one motif, art deco, can spawn so many different visions.

I flip through more pages and stop at a bright pink flapper-style dress in silk. The shift style hangs simply to mid-thigh, but the delicate design is accented with skinny spaghetti straps, while a feathered skirt adds femininity. I'm not normally a fan of feathers, but this dress looks adorable. My stomach grumbles, and I check the wall clock. Almost one o'clock! Somehow it doesn't surprise me that it's past lunch and Taylor has yet to make an appearance. I think of sneaking away for a bagel or something, but I just know that's the moment Taylor will decide to show herself.

Note to self, I think, *bring snacks to work*. I bargain with myself. *One more prototype, then knock on Taylor's door.*

I scope out some additional designs and get another brainstorm. Taylor didn't ask me to do accessories, but one of the dresses gives me the best idea for an art deco-inspired evening bag. If I get that done and a dress, that should definitely ease her grumpiness.

First things first: stay on task. I work on a sketch of a body-hugging top and free-flowing skirt. The bodice is strapless with shimmering geometric lines and metallic threading, while the white silk skirt is long and loose, flowing down past the ankles. The look is complete with a sheer headscarf, embroidered with pearls.

I pin the minidress to the mood board and stretch my shoulders. Still no sign of Taylor. That gives me time to

SILK CHARMEUSE
CAP-SLEEVED GOWN

EVENING BAG
DESIGNS

FLAPPER-STYLE
SILK DRESS

design the bag. I draw the silver chain first, taking care with each tiny oval. Then I sketch the clam-shaped bag. I envision the bag covered in white tile beads that shimmer under the light.

When I'm finished sketching, I get out of my chair and step back to admire my work. It's been a long morning, but I'm really pleased with the designs and the progress I made. My head is starting to hurt, though, so I knock on Taylor's door.

Taylor opens it, looking frazzled. "What's up?"

"I've done a lot of prototypes and wanted you to take a look," I reply.

Taylor blinks. "You've been working this whole time? But it's past two o'clock! You have to make sure you take lunch breaks. Especially since you're a minor." She looks worried.

I stare at her. Didn't she say she was going to check on me? Was I allowed to take a break?

Taylor moves past me and looks at my work. "These look exquisite," she says after a few minutes. "I can only imagine how stunning the finished products will be." She picks up my drawing of the evening bag. "You did this too?"

I nod.

"Very nice, Chloe. I'll send it over to handbags. I think they can do a lot with this design."

"Thank you so much," I say. I try to smile, despite my pounding headache.

"I'm sorry I forgot to touch base," Taylor says. "Take a long lunch. I don't need to be showcased on one of those blogs about horrible bosses."

I laugh. "Your rep is safe with me."

Taylor smiles. "Thanks for all your hard work, Chloe. I mean it. It's been such a pleasure working with you. I don't ever get sentimental about interns, but I'm actually sad you'll be leaving when the summer is over."

"Thank you for letting me be so involved in the process," I say. "So, what's next for the line?"

"Tomorrow will be similar to today, so don't forget to stock up on bagels and snacks in case you have to take a late lunch," Taylor advises. "Then we'll be working with Liesel McKay to finish the new additions. Oh, but I guess you won't be here then. That's next week, so you'll be on to your next rotation."

I'm curious which department I'll be in next week, but I'm disappointed I won't get to collaborate with Liesel. "Bummer. I was hoping to work with Liesel."

Taylor winks. "Just one perk of being a head designer," she says. Then she glances at the clock. "You really need to eat. Seriously." She goes back to her office but stops at the door. "The next two days are probably going to be crazy busy. So if I don't get to give you a proper goodbye, I'm saying it now."

"Thanks," I say, smiling. I might be starving, but I'm feeling so happy about Taylor's words of encouragement that it helps quiet my stomach's protests. Pleasing her seemed like no easy feat, and yet I managed to do just that!

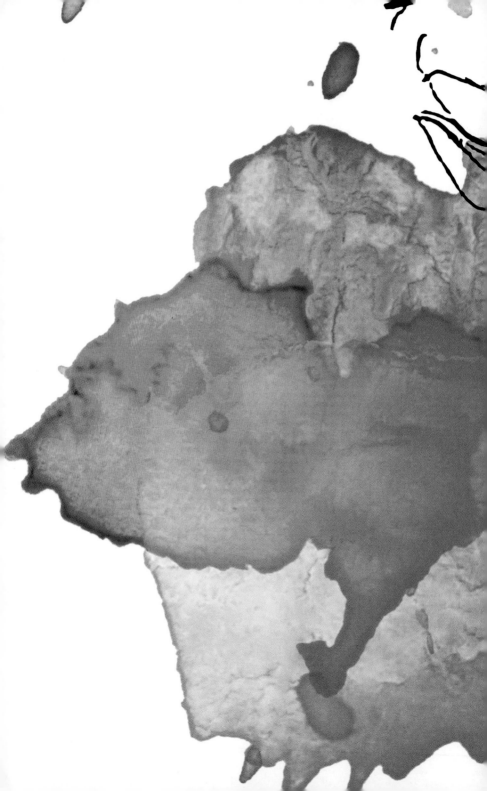

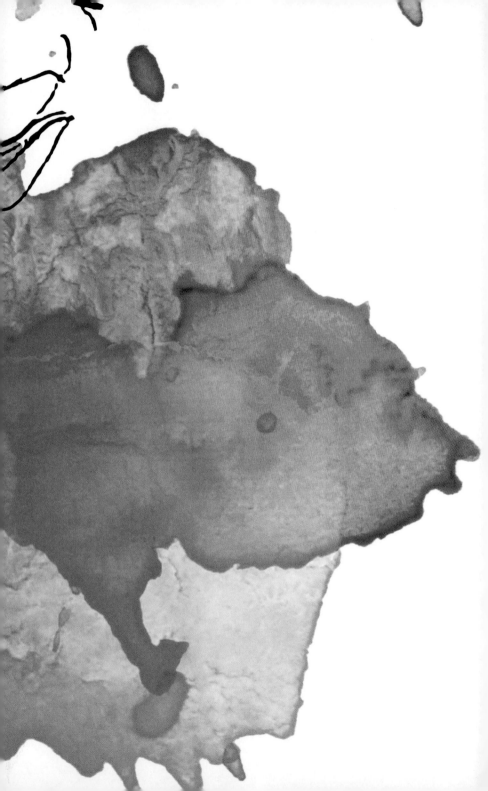

Taylor wasn't kidding about the next few days being crazy busy. I usually make it to lunch by one o'clock, but I remember to keep bagels and snacks at the ready in case I get hungry earlier.

I'm hoping for a bit of a reprieve when I arrive at Laura's office Thursday morning, but as soon as I see her, I can tell it will be another busy day.

"No time for hellos," Laura says as soon as she sees me. "Lots to do today." She rushes into her office, motioning for me to follow. I trail after her and notice all the new samples of collars she's created on top of her desk.

"I've been adding designs all week," Laura continues, "and I think we're good to go. Today we're working on knit skirts and dresses. Also part of Stefan's new art deco addition to Fashion Week."

"Sounds good," I say as Laura rummages through her desk. All the while, she's muttering about not having enough time to do anything.

Stress fills the room, and I have a sudden urge to swat at the air around me so her anxiety doesn't latch onto me. I don't need more. Since my internship started, I've felt like Laura on many days, but I'd never voice it. How can I be anything but one hundred percent excited and grateful about this opportunity? I mean, what high school student gets to intern in New York City — and for a famous designer at that?

I feel so lucky, but I'm also starting to miss home. I miss hearing about my best friend Alex's life and gossip. I miss kicking back and scarfing down junk food while watching bad television. I miss my parents. I miss —

"Chloe!" Laura's exasperated voice brings me back.

"Sorry," I say.

She waves her hand dismissively. "No time for that, either. Just focus, please." She pauses. "I'm sorry. It's easy to forget how young you are. I bet all this can be a lot sometimes."

I'm so grateful she gets it, but I don't want to admit there's something I can't handle. Still, I trust Laura.

"Sometimes," I admit quietly. "Not that I don't love it here," I quickly add.

Laura smiles. "It can be a lot for me too, and I've been doing this for years! Plus, I'm getting paid. Don't worry. You're doing great."

I feel a little better — definitely more relieved. It's hard walking around feeling guilty because you don't love every second of your dream job. It's a little scary too.

"Sooo . . . knits," says Laura. "The art deco movement is open to interpretation, but it relies heavily on bold geometric shapes, converging lines, and block patterns. Gold or silver threading throughout is common too. Some designers do bold colors, but Stefan prefers to keep them softer. He'd love to see green and rose in some of the designs."

Laura shows me some pictures of floor-length dresses with metallic threading. Another photo is of a skirt with a large diamond pattern. "These are some designs Stefan sent over," she explains. "I'm working on a few of my own designs as well. But what would be really helpful is if we could brainstorm and come up with some together. Listening to others always sparks my creativity. How does that sound?"

I love collaborating with Laura. "Perfect!"

* * *

Beside me, Laura sketches a design that reminds me of the black wool minidress from my trip to the Met. But rather than moons, Laura's dress has overlapping oval and leaf designs, along with a cowl neck.

"That's really pretty," I say. "It reminds me of Rudi Gernreich's designs."

Laura beams. "He's a real inspiration."

I study the sketch, which is primarily black, white, and gray, but notice that Laura has woven in shades of green as an accent. When she said to include rose and green, I'd imagined them as the primary colors. But I like her version better.

Laura continues perfecting her design, and I get a brainstorm. I draw designs similar to Laura's but with different collars. Instead of the green, I play with other colors like red, blue, and turquoise.

Beside me, I notice that Laura has stopped sketching and is watching what I'm doing. "I love those," she says. "Especially how the turquoise makes the dress pop."

"Thanks," I reply. "Your accents with the green gave me the idea."

The white pages of my sketchbook beckon for more designs, and I rub my temples, hoping to bring something to the forefront. I start making random lines and circles and envision them coming together to form . . . something.

I move the paper away from me to view the sketch in a new light. Then it hits me. With each pencil movement, the shape begins to form something cohesive. Soon, I'm looking at a tank dress with a scalloped bottom hem.

Laura glances at my design. "I like that a lot, but it needs something," she says. "Try adding metallic threading throughout."

"That's it!" I say. That's what was missing.

Laura taps her pencil on her chin and frowns at her sketchpad. She's drawn a fitted, knee-length dress with a wide boat neck and an empire waist. It's a beautiful, if simple, sketch.

"What else does it need?" Laura asks.

"Something to add some drama," I suggest. "What about making it floor length instead of knee length? You could add a pleated drop-waist skirt."

Laura lightly sketches the skirt I suggested and brightens. "Perfect!" She then uses colored pencils to add color to the dress, making a note to use silk charmeuse fabric.

"This is the most fun I've had in a long time," I say.

Laura grins at me. "I'm so glad," she says. Just then, her phone buzzes. She checks the text and sighs. "Stefan's on his way."

"Was he supposed to come today?" I ask. I hate being in the dark.

Laura shrugs. "It was possible, but I wasn't sure. I didn't want to stress you out."

She's right. I totally would have been stressed out.

"It will be good, don't worry," says Laura. "We can show him the sketches and get feedback immediately."

My interactions with Stefan have been positive, and he even called my pocket designs "impressive" at my first all-department meeting with him. Still, I get anxious wondering if he'll like the new designs. Laura was right to not tell me about the meeting ahead of time.

"Immediate feedback," I say. "Terrific."

Laura claps her hands, either not getting or ignoring my sarcasm. "Wonderful! And while he's here, this will be a great time to talk about the next phase of the internship."

I nod but don't say anything. The past two weeks have been so busy that I don't know if I can handle adding another department to the mix. But I seriously doubt Stefan will want to hear that.

ART DECO FASHION *Design*

TEAMWORK: COLLABORATION WITH LAURA

BOAT NECKLINE

PAINTED FABRIC

FITTED BODICE

Peach Silk Charmeuse

FITTED SKIRT

DROP-WAIST PLEATED BOTTOM

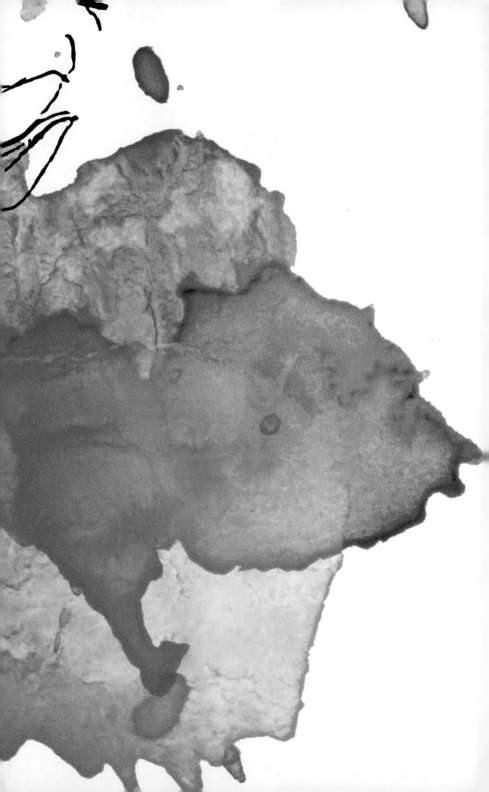

25

Laura flips through our designs while we wait for Stefan. "I like these," she finally says, "but Stefan's opinion is what matters."

"Sure," I say, as if her words don't make me nervous at all.

"I really do think he'll like them," says Laura.

"What will I like?" Stefan asks, poking his head in the doorway.

Laura jumps up from her chair, banging her knee in the process. "Good to see you," she says. "Chloe and I worked on some sketches today, and I was just telling her I think they're right up your alley."

Stefan steps closer. "Well, let's take a peek," he says. He hums as he looks through our sketches but doesn't say anything.

I try to catch Laura's eye, but she's too busy watching Stefan. He looks at each design three times and makes notes on the white space next to each drawing.

"I'm impressed, Laura," Stefan finally says. "I like the green accents here and the metallic touches. And the turquoise is lovely."

Laura smiles at me. "That one is Chloe's."

Stefan raises his eyebrows. "Good work, Chloe. I'll be honest, when we agreed to do *Design Diva*, I didn't know who we'd be getting. But you've really surprised me — in a good way."

"Thank you," I say gratefully. "It's been such a pleasure working here."

Stefan chuckles. "Well, don't say that just yet. There's more in store for you."

I try to laugh too, but my throat is dry.

"Let's discuss some of these designs," Stefan says. "I like that you understand the concept of art deco. And I know what you've been working on with Taylor, so it's great to see the range."

I'm floating on air, but I don't want to get my hopes up. I can sense a "but" coming.

"However," he continues, "Laura will work with you to refine your drawings. I definitely see where you're going with these, though, and I like the direction. Laura's leaf design is a favorite, and I'd like to see prototypes in turquoise and pale rose. Also, I'd like to see it as a shift. Make sense?"

"I think so," I say, glancing over at Laura. She nods.

"Good. I want to see prototypes of the other designs too," Stefan says. "Play with the sleeves — sleeveless, thin straps, cap sleeves. Give me options. I think they will fit in nicely with my vision for the knits I want to showcase."

"Wow, thanks so much, Mr. Meyers," I gush. I hold out my hand to shake his, feeling a little silly, but I'm not sure what else to do. Stefan Meyers himself just told me he likes my designs! Sure, he wanted changes and told me I can refine my work, but for once I'm not focusing on the negative.

Stefan rubs his chin. "You're doing so well here, it's a shame to move you."

"So don't," Laura chimes in quickly. "Seriously, I need her."

"Well . . ." Stefan says slowly. "The majority of Taylor's designs *are* set, and she'll be spending the next two weeks working with Liesel McKay. And I can see that the knits need more attention, and Laura can benefit from your assistance." He clasps his hands together. "Here's what we'll do. We'll keep you with Laura on the same days, Thursday and Friday. And you'll be with Michael in PR on Monday, Tuesday, and Wednesday. I think that's fair."

I relax. I'll be learning something completely new, but at least I'm only shuffling between two departments, not three.

"Perfect," Laura says with a smile. It's hard to tell what she's thinking, and I wonder whether or not she really believes that. "Good by you, Chloe?"

It's nice that she's asking, but we all know it has to be good by me. "Definitely, but, um, I'm not quite sure what PR does."

"You'll learn," Stefan says. "All the interns love it. It's glam with a capital G. PR is the brains behind making the Stefan Meyers label look good. You'll work with media contacts to get the word out about our spring line and what's ahead. You'll meet with reporters, you'll learn how to write pitches. Do some treks to *Vogue*. You may even chat up a few celebs. It will be unlike anything you've ever done!"

Stefan sounds so enthusiastic, I can't help but get excited too. Celebs? Alex would die! Media? Talking to the press? And *Vogue*? The thought of walking those floors is indescribable. "That sounds amazing," I say.

"It will be," Stefan agrees, "but it's going to be a lot of hard work too. I'm smart to only talk up the glam." He laughs.

"Speaking of hard work . . ." says Laura.

Stefan looks at his watch. "Understood. I'll be in touch. Best of luck, Chloe."

When Stefan leaves, Laura dives right into explaining how to fix the designs. "I know sometimes you only hear the negatives," she says. "So I want to stress how impressed both Stefan and I are with your drawings. That said, let's discuss how we can make them better."

I pull my chair closer to listen.

"First," says Laura, "you want to exaggerate your figures further. Elongate the neck for a more elegant look." She does a sketch beside mine, showing me how to exaggerate the figures.

"Another thing you should try," she continues, "is a black pencil to really define the drawing. Grays are nice, but blacks make for crisper lines." On her sketch, she outlines it in black, and I see the difference immediately.

I've been making fashion illustrations for years, but I'm excited by her suggestions on how to make them cleaner and better. "I've seen some people sketch on laptops too," I say.

Laura nods. "I prefer paper, but laptops can be really useful. Check this out." She takes my notebook to a scanner and copies the image. Then, she shows me a file on the laptop and opens it in Photoshop. It's my drawing!

"Cool!" I say.

"The computer makes it easy to erase any imperfections and clean it up. See these stray lines and smudges?" Laura says, pointing to a few spots where I erased.

I nod. "Yeah."

"Now watch," Laura says. In seconds, just by touching a few keys, the marks are gone.

"That's awesome!" I say. "Now my designs can look even more professional."

"I'd like you to use some of these ideas, and work on a sketch of the shift dress Stefan mentioned," says Laura.

I start drawing and think about what Stefan said about PR. How will I explain each design to the press? Will I get to meet Anna Wintour? I use a black pencil to give my drawing more definition, but my mind starts to wander. It's hard to stay focused when all I see are the pages of *Vogue* magazine — filled with my designs.

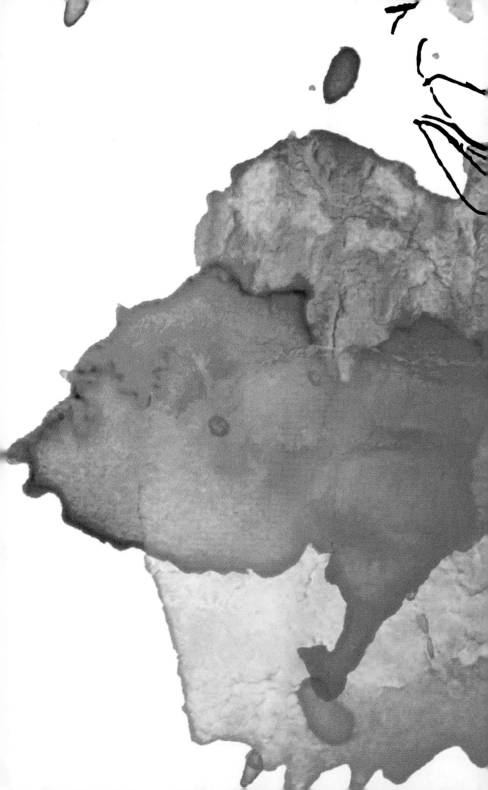

Dear Diary,

I can't believe I'm already done with the first month of my Stefan Meyers internship! I only have a month left until it's time to head back to my real life in California — more importantly, though, there's only three weeks to go until Fashion Week!

Everything is business as usual with my roommates: Avery and Bailey are sweet and fun, and Madison is still acting like she has it out for me, just like she has since day one. No matter what I do, she acts like I don't belong here because I won my internship on *Teen Design Diva*.

But back to the important stuff — Fashion Week. It has all my roommates on edge. Bailey keeps telling me, "Until everything comes together, it'll be total chaos — like a tornado, monsoon, and hailstorm combined." I'm trying to stay calm, but Bailey has interned before and knows the business better than I do, so her doomsday thinking is freaking me out just a little.

I already have enough to worry about without the added stress. I've been rotating departments every two weeks at work. So far, I've been in knits with Laura and dresses with Taylor. Tomorrow I start in public relations with Michael — for part of the week, anyway. Laura needs me too, so I'll work with her on Thursday and Friday and spend the other three days with Michael. Supposedly PR is super glam and can include working with the *Vogue* crew and dealing with the media. It's thrilling, but it's also a lot of pressure. I just hope I don't mess something up.

I mentioned all this to Alex when I talked to her on the phone, and she told me to go with the flow. And when I talked to Jake, he said the same thing. Easy for them to say! But both of them have been my cheerleaders since this whole thing started, so maybe they're right. Maybe I need to relax and go with the flow . . . but for now, I'd better get some sleep. Big day tomorrow!

Xoxo — Chloe

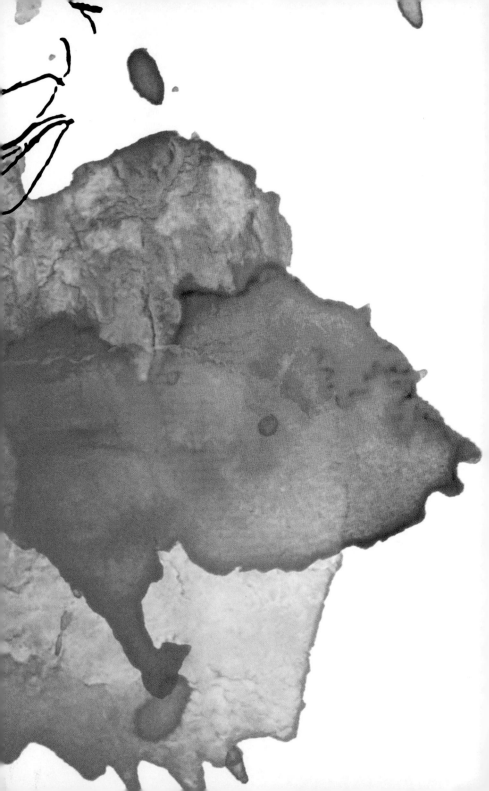

On Monday morning, I stand in front of the mirror and give myself the once-over. Since Stefan said PR is all about glitz and glam, I'm using today as an opportunity to wear one of the outfits I created during the *Teen Design Diva* competition — my final winning design. I slip into the monochromatic tailored shift dress, complete with metallic accents, and do a spin in front of the mirror.

Once I get to the Stefan Meyers headquarters, though, my nerves get the best of me. Every time I start to feel comfortable in a department, it's time to embark on a new challenge. I wish Laura, Taylor, or even Stefan were here to make today's transition easier.

I take a deep breath and open the door to the lobby. *You got this, Chloe*, I tell myself.

"Good morning, Miss Montgomery," says Ken, the security guard.

"Good morning," I say, showing my ID card.

Ken's familiar face usually puts me at ease, but today my stomach is participating in a full-on gymnastics competition. I pull out my phone and check the e-mail Stefan sent me with instructions, then head to the elevator and press the button for the twelfth floor.

When the elevator stops at my floor and the doors slide open, I'm shocked at what I see. Laura's and Taylor's departments had inspiration boards, mannequins, and fabric in every corner, but they were relatively quiet. People were either cutting material, sketching, or measuring garments. This floor is more organized, but it's *loud*. Everyone is either on the phone or typing something on the computer or shouting to someone else.

I glance at the e-mail, but it doesn't say where I can find Michael. "Excuse me," I say to a woman in one of the cubicles, "is Michael here?"

"One sec," she says. At almost the same moment, someone with a British accent says, "I'm right here."

I spin around. The man facing me has black hair that's tied back neatly in a ponytail. His warm amber eyes twinkle when he smiles. "I'm Michael Travers," he says, extending his hand.

"Chloe Montgomery," I reply, shaking his hand.

"Nice to meet you, Chloe," Michael says. "I've heard good things about you so far. I'm looking forward to working with you."

"Me too," I say. His accent sounds so proper, I feel like I should be watching my grammar or something.

"Splendid." Michael claps his hands. "What do you know about PR?"

I feel dumb already. All I know is that Stefan said something about glamour and celebs. "Um . . . not much," I admit.

Michael grins as though that's the greatest news he's ever heard. "That's wonderful! Truly wonderful!" he says. "The worst is an overly confident college kid who thinks he knows more than I do. You, my dear, are a blank slate."

"Um, thanks?" I'm glad he finds my ignorance useful.

"Don't be embarrassed," Michael says. "I'm here to teach you." He leads me into his office and motions for me to sit in one of the empty chairs. "Sorry for the mess."

Michael's definition of mess is very different from mine. All the papers on his desk are neatly organized into piles, his trash is nowhere near overflowing, and his coffee cup is resting on a coaster. There are dressers lining the office from door to window, each one chock full of Stefan's dresses, pantsuits, and denim items. I'd take a mess like this any day. If Laura had an office that looked like this, she'd be thrilled.

"It's amazing," I say.

"I suppose, but all this stuff is driving me batty." He sighs. "Thank goodness you'll be helping me with some of it today."

I'm confused. "Did you want me to organize all this for you?"

Michael looks surprised. "Goodness, no! This is as organized as it's going to get. You'll be assisting with clothing transport. It's not a very teachable moment, I'm afraid, but it's a necessity."

"Transport to where?" I ask.

"We've secured a placement in *Vogue* for some of Stefan's new pieces," Michael explains, "but I just received an e-mail saying they need the designs today instead of next week."

"Oh, wow," I say.

"I know — tight deadline," Michael agrees. "We'll start by going through these racks. I'll pick out five pieces that will show well, and then I'll be sending you to Laura and Taylor to pick up additional garments. Normally, we package and send things over. But because of the tight deadline and our proximity to *Vogue*, we'll get them ready, and you'll carry them yourself. Clear?"

I nod. The thought of my arms loaded with heavy clothes as I walk the streets of New York City is slightly overwhelming. I become extra conscious of today's outfit. It's perfect for dinner at an upscale club. Trudging through the heat, saddled like a mule? Not so much.

Just then Michael notices my heels. "Tell me you have other shoes," he says, sounding concerned.

I shake my head. "Not with me."

"Then let's hope those are more comfortable than they look."

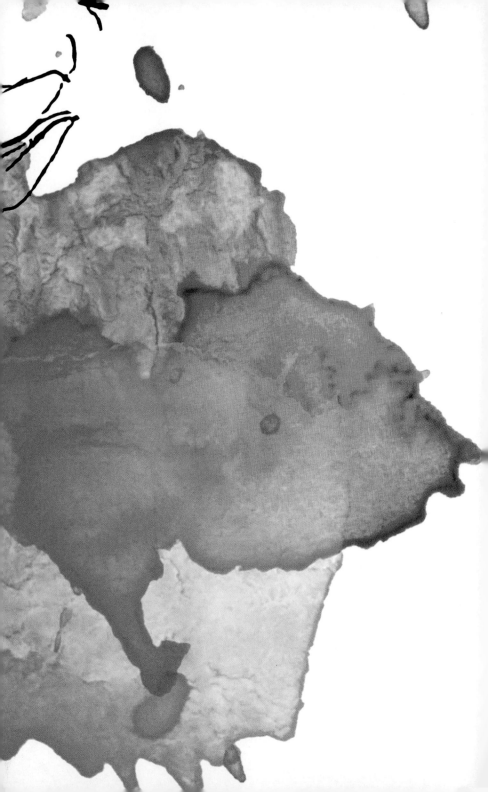

An hour later, my arms are loaded with two pairs of patterned jeans, a denim blouse with a velvet collar, and two dresses with embroidered pockets — pockets I designed! Michael had everything packaged in garment bags for easier transport, but they still weigh a ton.

My next stop is Laura's office. When I arrive, she has several garment bags all ready to go.

"Nothing like tight deadlines," Laura says. She unzips each bag to show me the pieces I'll be carrying, including an art deco-patterned sweater dress and a pantsuit. "It was really difficult to choose which designs to showcase since Stefan wanted to incorporate so many into Fashion Week. But we managed to part with a few he won't be showing."

I study the garments again. I don't see anything I've worked on, which is disappointing. But maybe that means some of the items I helped with are being saved for Fashion Week. I can only hope.

"Do you think I'll get to work with the stylists at *Vogue*? Will Anna Wintour be around?" I blurt out.

Laura's sympathetic face makes me feel silly. "Stefan talked up PR too much," she says. "There will be some cool stuff too, don't worry. But fashion isn't all glamorous. Remember when you sorted the closet on your first day here? It got better, right?"

I laugh. "Right. See you Thursday!"

"Counting down the days!" Laura calls as I leave her office.

Taylor is my last stop. As usual, her hair is pulled back in a bun, and she looks cool, calm, and collected. Her desk is covered with pieces of gold jewelry cascading down like a waterfall. I wonder if that's part of her Fashion Week collaboration with Liesel McKay, my former *Design Diva* mentor and Jake's mom.

"I have everything ready for you," Taylor says, not getting up from behind her desk.

I spot a bag with five hangers sticking out the top sitting on a nearby chair and shift the garments Michael and Laura gave me to my other arm. The weight is bearing down on me, and my toes are starting to look like sausages.

Very attractive, Chloe, I think.

I open the bags to take a peek, and my breath catches when I see the beautiful silk dresses I worked on. The last time I saw them, they were only prototypes; now they're full-fledged garments. The sparkly beading on the bodice of one of the pieces glistens in the light.

"Thanks," I say, grabbing the bag and heading for the door.

Taylor looks up from her work, then glances down at my feet. "You have no other shoes with you?"

I groan. I hope my cute gold heels don't become a death sentence for my feet. "Unfortunately not," I say.

Taylor raises an eyebrow. "Bring flip-flops from now on." With that piece of advice, she hunches back over her jewelry.

* * *

The sun beats down on me as I make the trek to *Vogue*. I shift the garment bags from one arm to the other and try to ignore the blisters on my toes and the sweat seeping down my dress. My phone buzzes, but I'm too loaded down to reach it.

I finally walk through the revolving doors and am hit with a blast of cool air. The security guard checks me in and doesn't even blink at my disheveled appearance. As I step into the elevator and ride it up to the eighth floor, a part of me still hopes to run into someone important. I imagine getting a tour of the office, seeing famous models up close, watching a photo shoot.

But my hopes are dashed as soon as the doors open and I see a girl not much older than me waiting. She smiles sympathetically. "I hope you didn't have a long walk. Life of an intern, huh?"

"How did you —" I start to ask, but the answer is pretty obvious. Who else would be lugging stuff across city streets?

The girl puts her arms out, and I hand over the bags, glad to be rid of them. "They're heavy!" she exclaims. Just then her phone rings, prompting an eye-roll. "My boss has texted me three times already. I don't know what she thinks I'm doing!"

Without another word, the girl waves goodbye and rushes off. So much for a *Vogue* tour.

The walk back to Stefan Meyers is much easier without the bags, but my toes are bleeding from my high heels, so I buy a pair of cheap flip-flops from a vendor and put them on.

My phone buzzes again, and I pull it out. I have two texts, both from Jake. The first is a photo of a soft pretzel, my favorite snack. The other says, "Can you tear yourself away from your glamorous life to have lunch with a commoner?"

I can't help but smile as I read his words. If only he could see me now. My flip-flops and throbbing shoulders are hardly the epitome of glam. I miss Jake, but the thought of putting on real shoes and walking anywhere makes my feet hurt even more.

"Dinner?" I text back.

"Class :-(" he replies.

I sigh and type "Rain check" as I rush back to the office to rest my feet.

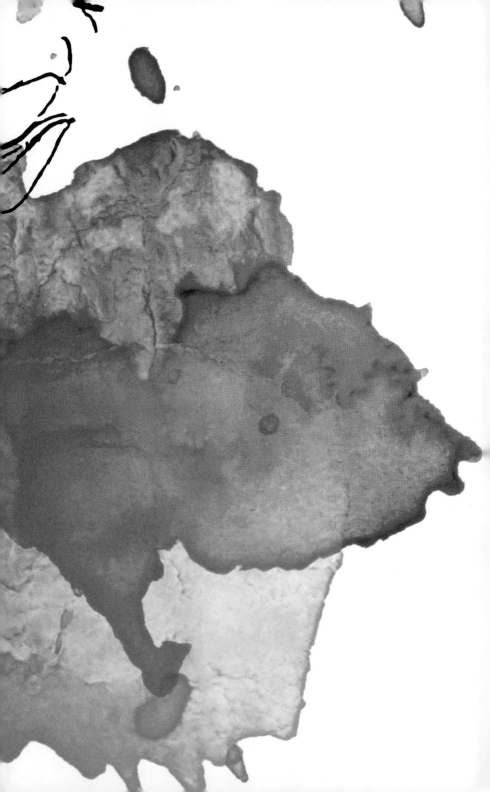

The next morning, my feet feel slightly more normal, and my bag is prepped with flip-flops. When I arrive at work, there's a cup of coffee already waiting at my desk.

"Is this yours?" I ask Michael, lifting the cup.

He chuckles. "No, my dear. That's for you. A thank-you for your hard work."

"This must be the glam part Stefan promised," I say.

Michael laughs. "You're funny."

I smile as I take a grateful sip. If today is anything like yesterday, I'll definitely need the caffeine.

"Today," says Michael, pulling a swivel chair up beside my desk, "you're going to learn about the press release and e-mail blast. Both are intended to get the word out about our brand. We want Stefan Meyers's styles to be seen everywhere — news media, magazines, newspapers, fashion networks."

I find myself leaning forward in my chair, caught up in his enthusiasm.

"The e-mail blast focuses on snappy facts and catchy headlines that will quickly grab readers' attention," he continues. "Journalists get hundreds of blasts a day, so ours needs to stand out. Even though the blast is more common, we do old-fashioned press releases too."

"Why?" I ask. I like the idea of short and snappy. It doesn't seem to make sense to bore people with something longer.

Michael beams as if my question is brilliant. "I love that you're thinking!" he says. "The longer press releases are perfect for new product launches. Say Stefan wanted to expand his brand into something he's never done before, like baby clothes."

I laugh. "I cannot imagine Stefan Meyers doing baby clothes."

"Exactly," says Michael. "Something so different would require more info. If an editor just saw 'Stefan Meyers Dresses Babies' as a headline, he'd think it was a joke. We also supply press releases to media outlets that prefer additional information when writing their stories. Some like the extra facts to bulk up their articles."

Michael goes into his office and comes back with a coffee for himself. "We'll start with the press release and then pull facts from that for the e-mail blast. What do you know about writing?"

"Like essays?" I say. I hate essays.

Michael laughs. "Hardly. Even with the longer press release, our goal is to create something that can wow in under a page."

I frown. Writing and I don't exactly mix.

"Don't worry," says Michael, reading my face. "We'll work on them together. First thing you have to do is forget what they taught you in school about writing."

I like this task! "Done!" I say with a laugh.

Michael grins. "Well, maybe not everything. You definitely want whatever we send to be free of grammatical errors. But don't worry about fancy vocabulary or a lot of description. The details have to grab the reader's attention quickly. Snappy titles are key too."

He shows me a template that says to focus on the five *w*'s — who, what, when, where, why — and the *h* — how. Our English teacher actually said the same thing, but I keep that to myself. "We'll focus this first piece on Stefan's spring line," he says.

"The *who* is easy," I say. "Stefan Meyers."

Michael writes that down. "Good."

"The *what* can be so many things, though," I say. "Denims, spring line?"

Michael taps his pencil on his chin thoughtfully. "Those are all good, but we want to wow. So what's the special line Stefan is working on?"

"Art deco!" I exclaim a little too loudly.

"Exactly," says Michael, writing that in the *what* column.

When and *where* are easy, and Michael fills in Fashion Week and Lincoln Center, respectively. "What about the *why*?" he asks.

I brainstorm out loud. "To bring back old-world glitz, the excitement of the Roaring Twenties, and to modernize old-style glamour?"

Michael writes down all my suggestions. "I like the last one a lot," he says. "We'll work on expanding that. That just leaves us with the *how*."

I check the notes on my laptop about the *w*'s and something clicks. "Does that mean the specifics of the fashion show? Explaining the looks and theme?"

Michael nods. "You got it."

I'm feeling more relaxed than when we started. Having this broken down with Michael makes it seem way less daunting.

"So what we have here is a great start, but it's just the bare bones," he says. "For the release, all these things have to be expanded. I've heard from Laura, Taylor, and Stefan that you have a great eye for fashion and really understand the new art deco line."

I blush. "Thanks."

"I want you to use that knowledge to expand on the *what*. Describe the fabric and cut of the pieces. Elaborate on the design. If you were trying to sell Taylor's dresses to someone, what would you focus on?"

This is more my speed. I take out my sketchpad and flip through the designs I did for Laura and Taylor.

"I'll let you get started on this on your own and come check up on you in an hour. Deal?" says Michael, handing me the notes he wrote. Now I can reference his and mine.

"Deal," I agree, eager to get into my design comfort zone.

Michael heads out, and I flip through my sketches, looking at my fabric descriptions. Taylor's dresses are silk and satin and feature unique details like hand-sewn beading. I also know the jewelry is handmade. I close my eyes, remembering the gold jewelry I saw in Taylor's office yesterday. It reminded me of cascading water. I scribble that in my notes and think about how to add attention-grabbing details.

When Michael stops by an hour later, I have a few solid paragraphs I'm proud of.

"Let's take a look," he says, pulling his chair closer. He reads my descriptions and smiles. "I like what you've done here. You really help the reader visualize the garments. It's clear you get Stefan's designs." He scrolls down. "Nice touch describing the jewelry piece as 'avant-garde.' And I like that you compared it to a waterfall. That's a nice image. I'll think about how to fine-tune this part where you describe the art deco style ranging from 'black-tie glamorous to daily chic,' but I like where you're going with it. Excellent for a first attempt."

"Thank you," I say. But there are still four more *w*'s and an *h* to tackle. "I didn't really know what to do with the heading and stuff."

"You have the hard part down," Michael says. "You know the designs and fabrics. The rest is easy." He goes into his office and returns with a binder. "I'm going to go over these old press releases with you, but I'll also let you take the binder home. I've also catalogued some of my favorite headlines from magazines and the industry. You can always learn from others. I'd like you to come up with at least three headline options for the press release. We'll use the same ones in the e-mail blasts, so we have to make sure they're eye-catching and sharp."

I flip through the binder. "I like this one about a basketball player's new shoe line," I say. "'Damian's Heart and Sole Endeavor.'"

"It's silly," says Michael. "But it gets your attention."

I look through more examples and stop at a reality celeb's clothing venture. "'Reassessing Frumpy Chic'?"

Michael laughs. "That design tanked, but the headline got a lot of people talking. Frumpy and chic don't go together at all, and people were dying to see the connection."

I think I'm starting to get the idea. The headlines can be funny or shocking or sophisticated, as long as they leave the reader wanting more. "This is a good one too," I say, "'Designers Revive Polka-Dot Sophistication.' I've never thought polka dots needed a revival or that they were sophisticated!"

"That's what I liked about it too," Michael agrees. "It was unexpected. Keep that in mind while you brainstorm. I look forward to seeing what you come up with."

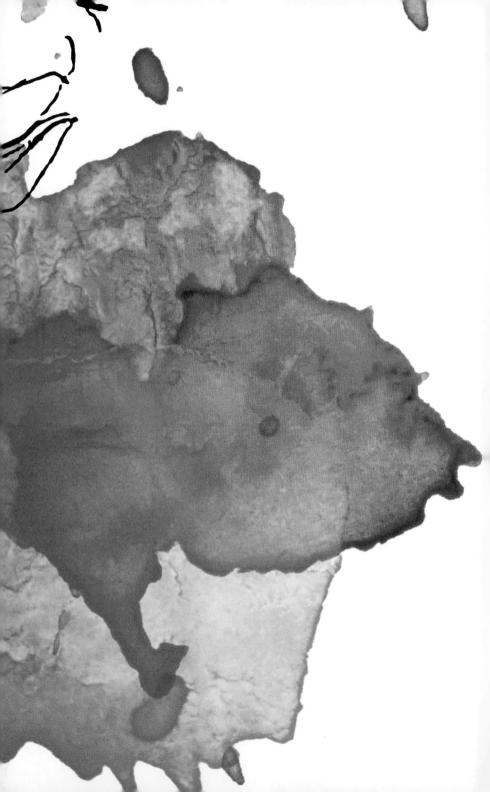

29

Wednesday morning, I have six headlines ready to go. I know, I know — overachiever much? But I want Michael to know I took this seriously. After all, writing isn't exactly my strong suit. I even took a stab at expanding the *who* portion of the release based on the information about Stefan in the binder.

Unfortunately, when I get to work, Michael seems too busy to be impressed. He breezes past me, sending papers flying off my desk. "It's going to be a crazy day," he says. Just then he notices the envelope I'm holding labeled PRESS RELEASE. "Oh, good, you finished! I can't wait to see it."

Michael takes the envelope and motions for me to follow him to his office. "You expanded the bio information!" he says, reading it over. "That's fabulous. And it looks like you managed to work in all the main points from the binder, including Stefan's award-winning fall line and his charity involvement. There are a few new updates to Stefan's career I didn't have in the binder, but I'll add them myself. Well done."

"Thanks," I reply, blushing a little.

Michael moves on to my headlines. The first one, "Stefan Unveils Art Deco Magic" was one of my first tries.

"It's good you mention the art deco upfront," Michael says, "but it doesn't say much. What does 'magic' mean, you know?"

I nod. That wasn't my favorite either, but I was hoping Michael would disagree. I guess they can't all be winners, though.

Michael keeps going down the list. "This is better," he says. "'Stefan Meyers Brings Back Roaring Twenties.' But I'm interested in *what* he's doing to bring that back. That's my hook."

That headline was one of my favorites, and I'm a little disappointed Michael isn't totally wowed by it.

"This one," says Michael, pointing to my last headline, "focuses on what Stefan wants to get out about his line. 'Stefan Meyers — Regal, Elegant, Art Deco Line.' It hints at what Stefan's line will be about without hitting readers over the head."

Michael rubs his chin. "Let's combine my two favorites. How about 'Stefan Meyers Brings Back Roaring Twenties with Elegant Art Deco Line.'"

"I love that!" I say, impressed at how quickly he was able to pull out the best parts of both headlines and turn them into something great.

"I'm going to finish fine-tuning the release," Michael tells me. "You, however, were promised glam. Today, you'll get to work on a project that should meet those expectations." He wheels a cart full of fashion and tabloid magazines over to me. "Are you familiar with these?"

Familiar? Alex and I have spent entire weekends flipping through magazines like these and dissecting each page. "I live for them!" I reply.

Michael laughs. "Breathe in as many as you can. That's today's task."

I stare at him, feeling confused. "You want me to read fashion mags all day?" I ask. That sounds too good to be true.

"Not just read," Michael explains. "I need you to scrutinize. I want you to peruse the pages and make notes of which celebs are wearing Stefan Meyers. Then, you'll scour celebrity Instagram accounts for the same thing. When you're done, we'll compile a list and use the information for publicity material. We'll know which celebrities to approach in the future about wearing our designs. Any questions?"

"Nope," I say quickly. Best. Assignment. Ever.

* * *

I spend the rest of the day taking notes, even eating lunch at my desk, but it's totally worth it. I make sure my information includes the celeb's name, the links or pages to the designs, and a description of the outfit worn.

I spot an image of Lola Corrigan, my favorite actress, in a tan suede jacket and black skirt and remember dragging Alex to the television so we could get a closer look when they dissected it on *Fashion Police*.

I find a shot of Hunter Bancroft, one of the *Design Diva* judges, wearing a pair of Stefan Meyers corduroy slacks. Each leg panel is done in a different color. It's just the type of out-of-the-box style Hunter enjoys, and he pulls it off.

I send a photo to Jake, knowing he'd never wear the design. His style is much simpler and more masculine. His mom might be a famous designer, but Jake is a jeans-and-T-shirt guy all the way.

"Your new pants?" I type.

I get a response right away. "If Hunter can wear them, so can I! :-)" Jake writes back.

"Hope to see that soon!" I reply. I really miss Jake. I thought I'd see him way more once I was in New York, but I've hardly seen him at all. I've just been so busy with my internship. And with Fashion Week fast approaching, I don't see that changing anytime soon.

"Me too! Miss you!" Jake texts.

I smile. It's good to know he feels the same way.

I flip through more accounts and stumble upon Cassie McRay, Alex's favorite basketball player, wearing a Stefan Meyers tankini. I had no idea Stefan had a bathing suit line! I love the bright colors on the suit and send a link to Alex.

I go through dozens of accounts and more than fifty magazines. When it's time to go home, I'm exhausted, but I'm also inspired. I think about what I would do if I had my own line. Would I focus on everyday and eveningwear or be more versatile, like Stefan? I guess only time will tell.

TAN SUEDE JACKET

FUNKY ACCESSORIES

BLACK PENCIL SKIRT

TANKINI

GOLD STILETTOS

RESEARCH
STEFAN MEYERS
Designs

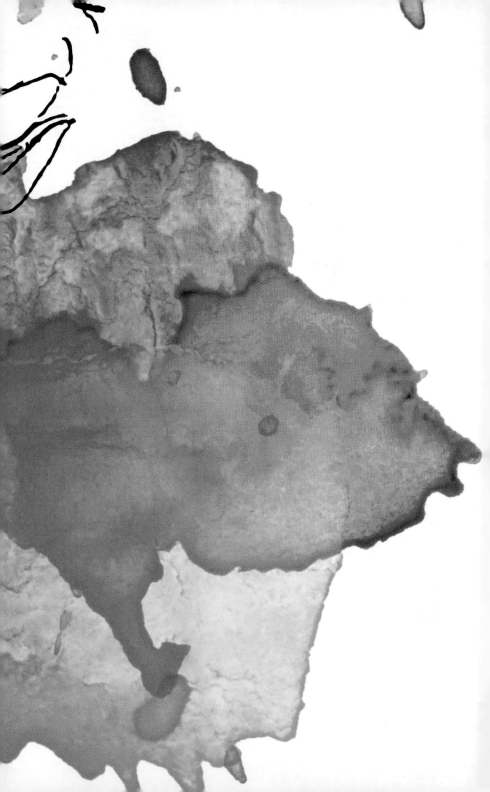

On Thursday, my first day back with Laura, I'm up bright and early. Sitting up in bed, I stick in my headphones, pick up my pencils and sketchpad, and start drawing.

I sketch wrap dresses with curved and plunging necklines in multiple colors. I add details to sleeves, hems, and collars like I've seen on some of Stefan's pieces. During *Design Diva*, I saw how tiny additions could really set a piece apart, and now, in the midst of the fashion industry, I'm noticing that even more.

Using a tan pencil, I color a pair of silky geometric-patterned shorts. I think about Stefan's art deco motif and shade in the shapes with a salmon pencil, then pair them with a solid-color blouse. A salmon-colored handbag with gold clasps completes the look.

IDEAS
AND
Designs

SOLID
SILK TOP

PATTERNED
SHORTS

HEELED
BOOTIES

SALMON
BAG

WRAP
DRESSES

Suddenly someone taps my shoulder, and I'm so startled I almost fall off the bed. I pull out my headphones and turn to see Avery standing there.

"Sorry, I didn't mean to scare you," she says. "Your door was open."

"That's okay." I look at the clock. "I should get going soon anyway. I don't want to be late."

"Where are you today?" Avery asks.

"With Laura," I reply. "I think she's finishing stuff for Fashion Week. I was in PR Monday, Tuesday, and Wednesday. How about you?"

"I'm in marketing and advertising now," Avery replies. "I really like it so far. I was watching you sketch, and you had this calm, happy look on your face. I'm not like that when I'm trying to design. It's so stressful! But with advertising, we have to do ad campaigns and think of slogans, and I love it. It just comes to me." She smiles.

"That's great," I say.

Avery looks relieved. "I know. I thought I messed up by choosing fashion as my major. It's a relief to see that there are other ways to work in this field. So much depends on how you present a piece to the world. I'm working on a campaign for 'chic sneaks' right now, and the goal is to show that the sneaker can be a workout shoe in one light, but dressy in another. We've gone through a few drafts of ad campaigns trying to make that balance obvious."

"My friend, Jake McKay, the one who came by the room before, is a marketing major too. Until he explained what he does, I never realized how important a campaign was, either! You really have to find the right buyer, huh?" I ask.

"Exactly," says Avery. "It's just such a relief to find my place!" She looks at her watch. "I'd better go, but thanks for chatting."

"See you soon!" I say, glad I could help. Avery is already in college and must have been scared when she didn't love every moment of her internship. We all have doubts, I realize.

I think again about how lucky I am to have this opportunity while I'm still in high school. I realize something else too. Not every part of an internship is a dream, but that's what makes it real.

* * *

"How's PR going?" Laura asks when I arrive at the office an hour later.

"It's cool!" I reply. "I love learning about the different departments. Yesterday, I got to look at magazines all day."

Laura's smile looks forced. Does she think I like working with Michael more than with her?

"Designing is still my passion," I reassure her. "I don't think all the glitz in the world will change that."

"Well, what I've seen so far has really impressed me. Let's put all that talent to good use." Laura winks at me and gets busy laying out prototypes.

There's a black blouse with white triangles. Another shirt is cotton with an art deco-inspired chevron pattern. Both items have smooth, mother-of-pearl buttons down the front.

"These are additions to Stefan's art deco line," says Laura. "He wants to add some menswear-inspired pieces for versatility. Notice the geometric patterns, which are key elements. I want you to study these prototypes. Then go on Stefan's website and take notes on his menswear as well. Pay special attention to the patterns, cuffs, and collars. Notice which he uses most frequently."

I nod. I can do that. I'm used to inspecting designs and taking note of common elements or what sets them apart.

"Once you've done that, I'd like you to take a stab at your own menswear-inspired sketches," says Laura.

I bite my lip. In all my years of designing, I've never created men's clothing. All my sketches were things I wanted to wear myself. "Um . . . I don't normally design men's stuff."

"That's okay — this is just menswear-inspired. Think about some masculine elements and how you could make them more wearable for women. We'll discuss them together when you're finished," says Laura. "You can do it."

Laura heads back to her office, and I pull up Stefan's site, still feeling a bit uncertain. I plow through page after page of menswear, making note of the slim fit that seems to be a constant through formal, sports, and office wear. I notice Stefan's signature buttoned barrel cuffs and variety of open collars.

Laura mentioned that Stefan wants these pieces to be part of the art deco collection, so I search online for images of men in the 1920s and 1930s. There are photos of men in braces — suspenders with buttons — and with pocket squares. I also notice a lot of hats — Panama hats, bowlers, fedoras — and pinstripes. Now I just have to translate those styles into something a modern woman would wear. Easy, right? Not.

My first few sketches, a mash-up of preppy and formal wear, find a home in the trash. In my head, the final product is stylish, but I can't seem to get the same result in my sketchpad. The next few drawings resemble something a kid would wear playing dress-up.

I try a different approach and sketch the items separately. Slim-fit shirts in a variety of patterns fill my pages. I add some wrap blouses to the mix for a more feminine silhouette, then add vintage-inspired and classic collars. Next, I play with the cuffs, making some barrel, others French. I add exaggerated cuffs to some of the wide-leg pants I've sketched as well.

Once I've nailed the shape, I move on to patterns, adding pinstripes to a sleeveless blouse. Another, I detail with converging silver lines. I experiment with only adding art deco elements to the pocket squares and braces, leaving the shirts solid.

Soon, my sketchpad is filled with a new section of menswear-inspired designs. I take them out to Laura's desk to show her what I've done, but she shakes her head, and my heart drops. I really thought I had nailed this assignment.

"Sorry," I say quietly. "I guess I missed the mark."

Laura looks surprised. "Not at all! I just didn't expect you to excel so quickly at this too."

What's that supposed to mean? I think. *Did she not want me to do well?*

The confusion must show on my face because Laura says, "That came out wrong. I can tell you're very talented, but when Stefan suggested you work on this, I was worried. I know you don't have much experience with men's clothing, and I was afraid you'd get discouraged.

You're a hard worker, Chloe, but you take a lot to heart. I didn't want you to get down on yourself."

I get what she means. My mom has had very similar advice for me in the past. "I know this internship is about learning, but I still want to be . . ." I search for the right word.

"Perfect?" Laura says with a laugh. "Honey, who is? If you keep measuring yourself by such high standards, you'll burn out before you've made a spark."

I sigh. "I know."

"But you did impress me," she continues. "It's clear you took your time with both the prototypes and the website. I like your variety of collars and patterns. And the silhouette of this wrap top is a great way to make menswear more accessible to women. The wrap really works well with the pinstripes — it helps soften the lines."

Laura flips through the sketches again. "I'd like to see these in more colors, and I want prototypes of the pinstripe blouse for the board. Nice work."

I head back to my desk, thinking about what Laura said about burning out. Striving for perfection is what got me here. How can wanting to succeed in everything be bad?

STRIPED PANTS

GOLD ACCENTS

New Black S

- PINSTRIPE
- cuffs
- collars
- Tailored

WAIST ACCENTS

killer cuffs

high collar

Feminine Colors?

MENSWEAR DEVELOPMENT Sketches

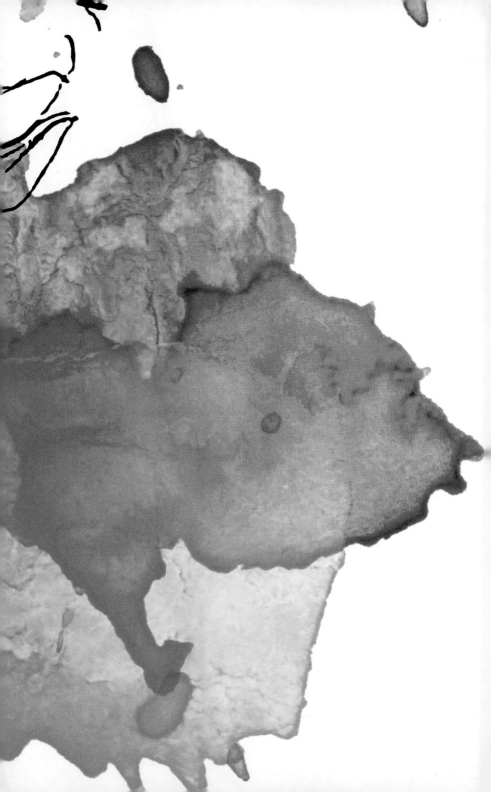

31

I'm with Laura again on Friday, and the day goes smoothly. I'm starting to feel more comfortable with the menswear-inspired pieces. I especially like getting lost in the fine details of the cuffs and collars. I even find myself noticing the shirts men wear. From the sporty to the dressy, they all have a unique fit.

As the day draws to a close, I think about Jake. We haven't seen each other in two weeks, and texting just isn't the same. Hopefully we'll get to hang out this weekend.

As if reading my mind, Laura says, "Michael would like you to see him. He has a weekend assignment for you."

I sigh. *Homework on the weekend? Really?* But I try not to be too upset. If this is what it takes to make it in the fashion world, there's no point in complaining.

Michael is waiting for me when I get to his office. "Do you know what market research is?" he asks.

241

"Uh, like researching the market?" I guess, going for the most obvious explanation. The truth is, I have no idea what this means.

Michael grins. "Exactly. Have it ready for me Monday!"

I panic. Is he serious?

Suddenly, Michael bursts out laughing. "Just teasing. Here's the deal — we're looking for you to see what's out there. Look at the items shoppers gravitate toward. Check out the trends, as well as what's on the clearance rack. Compare other designers' prices with ours. If something catches your eye, sketch it. Don't try to analyze why you're drawn to it, or you might miss something."

I perk up. This is unlike any homework assignment I've had before. "Do you want me to take notes on specific lines or designs?"

Michael shakes his head. "Nope. I don't want you to think too hard. I want to see what *you* think is important. You'd be surprised what we can learn this way."

"But I don't know this industry like you do," I say. "What if I miss something?"

"Your inexperience is precisely why you're perfect. You'll view items from a different perspective than a professional. A less-experienced eye might pick up on a detail or a trend that someone else would pass over," says Michael.

I've never thought of it that way, but it makes total sense. "Can I take pictures?" I ask. I imagine lurking behind displays and sneaking photos of different outfits.

"That would be helpful," Michael says, "but most stores no longer allow that because of security issues. Better to sketch instead."

My face falls. "I liked thinking of myself as a spy," I say sheepishly.

Michael's face grows serious. "You still are. We're counting on you to report back with valuable information. Here are your instructions and the stores to hit." He gives me a large manila envelope. "Agent Chloe Montgomery, will you accept your assignment?"

I hold back a smile. "I will."

* * *

"Going to rob a bank?" asks Madison when she sees my outfit Saturday morning.

I roll my eyes. Maybe I've taken this spy thing too far, but it's too fun not to! I'm dressed in a black romper and have a black scarf tied around my neck. The black sunglasses might be overkill, though. "You never know," I say.

She stares at me, getting unnerved because she can't see my eyes. "Whatever," she finally says. "Have fun."

I grab my bag, fling open the door, and jump when I see Jake standing there, hand poised to knock.

"Hey!" I say, giving him a hug. "What are you doing here?"

"We didn't make definite plans, and I missed you. I thought I'd surprise you." He looks me over. "Going somewhere?"

"Kind of, but you should come! I'm doing market research — it's so up your alley." I fill him in on my assignment as we walk outside. "Michael, one of my bosses, gave me a packet with information. I'm supposed to start with one of the high-end stores: Bergdorf, Henri Bendel, Barneys. He also gave me a charge card with instructions to bring back at least three of my favorite designs."

I've passed the stores on Michael's list several times, but I've never gone in. Even if I had, it's not like I could have afforded to buy anything. Today will be different. If only school was this exciting!

"After you, m'lady," says Jake, holding open the door to Barneys.

I giggle. "Why, thank you, sir."

Walking into Barneys is like walking into another world. The floors look like they're made of marble, and there's a beautiful winding staircase that looks like it belongs in a mansion. And then there are the displays.

Each item is hung perfectly. The shoes in the shoe department are arranged by color scheme, size, and heel height. The lighting surrounds them like a halo, showcasing each heel and strap in the best possible angle.

I think of department stores back home. There are always shoes left on the floor or shirts thrown on racks. I've even tripped over a pair of pants left in the middle of the floor.

I grab Jake's hand and we take the escalator to skirts. One item immediately catches my attention. I sketch its contrast trim and rounded hem. I expect the zipper to be in the back, but it's hidden in the front. The shirt it's paired with isn't really my style, but it's certainly unique. I sketch the silk material and tiny polka dots, then add the gold and black design on the front.

I turn to show Jake a sketch, but he's nowhere to be seen. I was so engrossed in my assignment that I didn't even notice he'd left.

"What do you think of this?" I hear him ask from a few racks down. He's holding up a dress with an argyle knit pattern.

"I like the mesh top panel and the tan and black together." I head over and check the price tag. Five hundred fifty-nine dollars! For rayon and spandex?

"How much would Stefan Meyers charge for something like this?" Jake asks.

I have no idea. For all I know, Stefan's clothing might cost even more. I sketch the dress, then make a note about the price.

As we walk through the racks, my book quickly fills with sketches of jackets and dresses. I make notes about the fabrics I see and the detailed embellishments. One of my favorites is an embroidered paisley dress with a deep V-neck. I take it with me to bring back to Michael and start sketching a satin blouse with rhinestones on the collar.

"Chloe? Chloe!" Jake says, sounding irritated.

"Huh?" I say, looking up from my sketchbook. "What's wrong?" Jake looks annoyed. He must have been trying to get my attention for some time.

Jake shakes his head. "I shouldn't have just stopped by. You're obviously busy. Let's catch up later." He gives me a hug goodbye and starts to walk away.

"Wait!" I say. "This won't take all day. I'm almost done." I show him my sketches.

"They're good," he says, "but don't you want what you present to Michael to be great? You should hit one more store at least." He doesn't look annoyed anymore, just a little sad.

I start to argue. I really want to hang out with him today, but I know he's right. I need to focus. Still, is it so selfish of me to want him to tag along? "Rain check?" I ask.

"Definitely." Jake smiles, and his adorable dimple winks at me. Then he's gone.

I stand there for a moment, feeling bummed. But there's no time to waste. I have work to do. I make a beeline toward the clearance rack, paying close attention to the marked-down clothes. A cropped black sweater catches my eye, and I imagine it paired with killer black boots. The price has been marked down five times, and it's only thirty dollars! I take one for myself and grab another for Michael. Then I sketch it, adding examples in other colors.

More clearance-rack sweaters beckon. I draw a sheer silver knit with an extended front hem as well as a forest-green sweater dress with beading around the collar. Before moving to the next department, I place both outfits in my bag for Michael.

In skirts and blouses, I follow a college girl who appears to have the same taste in clothing I do. At one point, she holds up a tailored, lavender shirt with mother-of-pearl buttons down the front. She looks in the mirror and checks the price tag before slowly putting it back on the rack. When she walks away, I sketch the shirt.

Finally I tear myself away from Barneys to check out another store. More than once, I think of turning and showing Jake one of my sketches, only to realize he isn't there. I comfort myself with visions of shopping and spying and head to Bendel's.

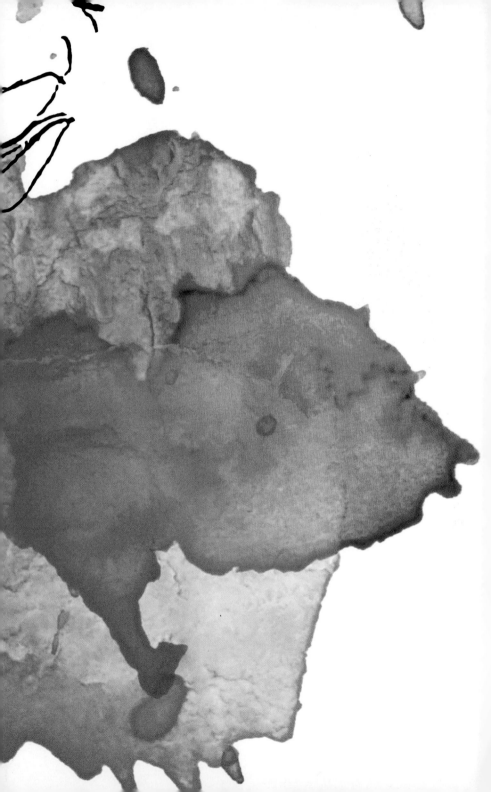

On Monday morning, Michael puts his legs up on his desk and takes a sip of coffee. "You like this knit style?" he asks, holding up my clearance sweater.

"I love it," I say.

Michael rubs his chin. "It's something to think about. I'll be passing all these drawings on to Stefan."

I wait as Michael examines the rest of my sketches. My shopping mission lasted all weekend. Sunday, I hit Bergdorf's. Whenever I caught myself missing Jake and wondering if I should have cut my shopping expedition short, I'd sketch another dress or pair of shoes. Losing myself in work is always easy.

"The spreadsheet you created of the prices makes comparing them that much easier. Seems like you had fun," Michael comments.

"Oh my gosh — so much!" I blush, remembering my little spy getup.

"Excellent! Because I have some online detective work for you next," Michael says. "I need you to compile a list of women's fashion blogs. You're looking for the blogs with the most followers. Read the comments to gauge readers' interests. Take notes on which blogs showcase the Stefan Meyers line. It'll help us keep tabs on who to contact for more promotions."

"Got it," I reply. I head to my desk and open my laptop. But before I can do anything, my phone buzzes with a text from Jake: "Rain check? 6? Frankenstein's Tavern?"

I type back quickly. "Yes!"

With one less thing to worry about, I dive into the blogs. I check the file Michael sent me of alerts with Stefan's name and make a spreadsheet of the blogs that mention him the most. I'm working on ranking the blogs according to the number of followers, then mentions of Stefan Meyers, when Stefan himself breezes past me. "Come, Chloe!"

Me? I think. I scramble from my seat and follow Stefan to Michael's office.

"I wanted to deliver this great news in person!" Stefan announces. I see Michael trying to hide his surprise at Stefan's sudden appearance. "*Teen Design Diva* wants Chloe to be a guest judge this season!"

"Really?" I say. I can't believe it!

Michael looks less than thrilled. "When?"

"Today," Stefan says excitedly. "It's such a great opportunity. To have our intern involved in the judging keeps the spotlight on Stefan Meyers, especially with Fashion Week only two weeks away! Talk about great PR!"

"It *is* great PR," Michael admits grudgingly. "But there's still so much I'd like Chloe to do *here*."

Stefan grins at me and waves off Michael's concern. "Chloe can handle it all, can't you?"

A little voice inside me panics. *PR! Laura! Fashion Week! And now judging? Don't forget your date with Jake!* I push the panic away. "No problem," I say, giving him a confident smile.

Michael turns to me. "How's your blog report coming?" He doesn't give me a chance to answer before he turns to Stefan. "When do they need her?"

Stefan looks at his watch. "She needs to report to *Design Diva* headquarters on 45th Street in an hour."

"An hour?" Michael sputters.

Stefan shrugs. "It was in a memo from two days ago, but I just saw it. Sure dodged a bullet, didn't I? We could have missed the whole thing!"

Michael grumbles something. "There's still so much to do. Finish the blog work, help with gift bags, see how we work with models, help out during the fashion show . . . the list goes on."

My mouth hangs open at all the opportunities ahead. Stefan wasn't kidding about glamour.

"The show is filming at the hotel you stayed in during the *Teen Design Diva* competition. You will be reporting to the conference room. Do you remember how to get there?"

I nod, remembering the hotel's marble floors and large conference room where we had to sew our designs. I'm excited but feel bad for leaving Michael.

"Tomorrow, it's back to the grind," I promise. "In the meantime, here's everything I've done so far." I hand him my blog spreadsheets and research.

"Have fun," Michael says reluctantly.

"Thank you!" I'm tempted to hug both him and Stefan but manage to control myself.

I leave the office with just enough time to stop in my dorm and spruce up my outfit, changing into a cute taupe dress with a black belt. If I'm going to be on TV again, I want to look my best!

The little voice in my head keeps nagging me about taking on too much, but I swat it away. Besides, Stefan made it pretty clear he wants me to go. It's not like I could have said no, even if I'd wanted to — which I didn't.

Just then, my phone buzzes with a message from Jake. "Can't wait to see you tonight!"

I think about telling him about my temporary *Design Diva* gig, but I'm sure I'll be done with the judging by then. "Me too!" I write back. Who says I can't do it all?

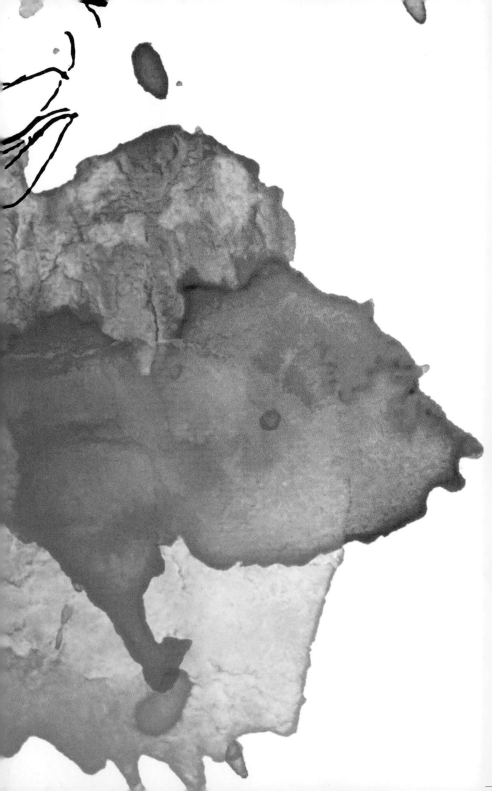

I pause at the entrance of the hotel where I completed so many challenges. *Teen Design Diva* seems ages ago. I take a deep breath and walk through the doors to the large conference room, pausing in the doorway to observe everything around me.

Contestants are sitting in groups, sometimes throwing nasty glances in their rivals' direction. The judges, Jasmine DeFabio, Hunter Bancroft, and Missy Saphire, are huddled in a corner, deep in conversation. Even though I'm not the one with designs on the line, the familiar butterflies return to my stomach.

Just then, Missy spots me. "Chloe!" she cries, running over with her arms outstretched.

Her outburst draws everyone's focus to me, and the contestants point at me and whisper to each other. They're probably wondering what the heck I'm doing here.

Missy pulls me in for a hug before dragging me toward the other judges. "Come, come."

Jasmine's warm smile catches me off guard. "Good to see you, Chloe."

"You look good," Hunter adds, his blue eyes twinkling. "Very chic."

I smooth down my ruffled dress, happy with the choice. "Thanks!"

"We're looking forward to hearing your thoughts today," says Missy. "It will be great for the contestants to get feedback from someone who's been there."

"I'm happy to help," I reply. "But . . . to be honest, I'm not sure what I'm supposed to do."

Missy smiles reassuringly. "You'll walk around with us, following our lead. You can ask questions about the designs, but don't give feedback — we don't want to clue them in to which way we're leaning. Once we start judging, feel free to express what you like and don't about the designs. Make sense?"

I nod. "I think so. But I don't want to discourage them during the judging process."

"Don't worry," says Hunter. "Everyone has his or her own style. You can be constructive without being discouraging. Maybe focus on what you like before you say how to make something better."

"That's a good idea," I say.

Jasmine glances at the clock, and her face takes on the stern look I remember. "People!" she calls to the contestants. "Please gather round. I'd like you to meet our guest judge, Miss Chloe Montgomery. I'm sure she has a few words she'd like to say."

I look nervously at Hunter, who nods encouragingly. I didn't think to have a speech prepared.

"Um," I begin. "I'm so excited to be here today. This show has provided me with an amazing opportunity, and I'm so lucky to have been a part of it." I pause and think about what helped me win. "Go with your heart. Don't worry about what someone else might say. Just design what you believe in."

The contestants clap, and I feel like a celebrity.

Missy raises her hand for silence. "Today we're going back in time to the decade of bell-bottoms, peace signs, and all things groovy," she says. "It's the 1960s, baby!"

My interest is immediately piqued. What a cool challenge to judge! There are so many possibilities. I'd take this over my first *Design Diva* challenge — animal-inspired clothing at the zoo — any day!

"Before you get carried away," Hunter says, "let me give you all the info. We're looking for pieces inspired by 1960s patterns or styles. But as with all our challenges, there's a catch. You'll need to incorporate two styles — and they must be pulled out of our hat." He reaches into a box on the judges' table and pulls out a velvet hat.

A girl with flaming red hair whose nametag reads Dani goes first. She closes her eyes, reaches into the hat, and swiftly pulls out a scrap of paper. "Op art and swirly patterns!" she calls out.

A boy with a rainbow Mohawk — Kyle, according to his nametag — is next. He takes a deep breath before slowly opening his assignment. "Tie-dye and fringe," he says. "Far out!" Everyone laughs.

A contestant with a lip ring, Carrie, walks up tentatively and draws out a slip of paper. "Peace sign and turquoise?" she says, then shuffles back to her seat. Those elements leave a lot of room for her to put her own spin on the piece. I'd have been excited, but Carrie looks confused.

The contestants continue coming up and choosing styles until all fifteen are done.

"I have some final instructions," says Jasmine. "Use this challenge as an opportunity to step out of the box. Don't make one big peace sign or flower and say that's your vision. I want to see more than that."

I stifle a giggle at Jasmine's command to think outside of the box. I heard that phrase more than once during my stint on the show. If only it offered more direction.

"You will have three hours to complete your design," says Missy. "At that point, we will discuss what you created. Then the judges will deliberate, and one of you will go home. Any questions?"

The contestants nervously look at each other. I remember that feeling. No matter how many times you go through the process, each elimination leaves you worried you'll be next.

"Ready?" says Missy. "Five, four, three, two, one — go!"

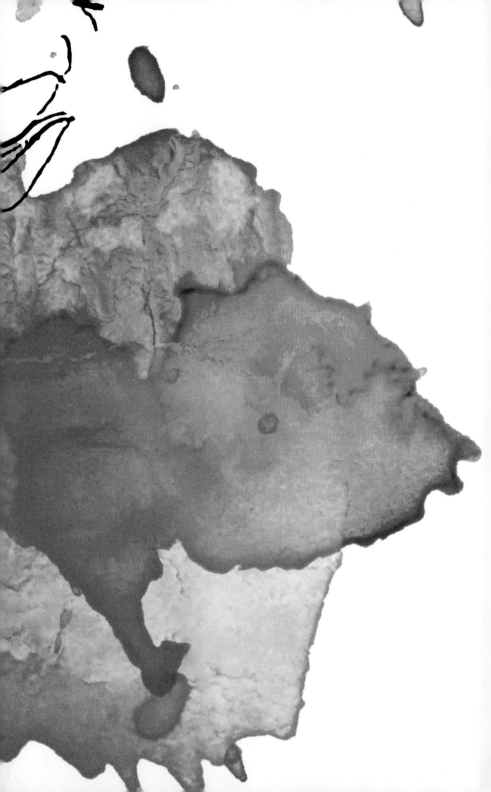

34

Just like when I was on the show, the contestants seem to be divided into two types of designers — those who run and grab the materials and those who take their time perfecting their vision.

I remember how crucial those beginning minutes were and give the contestants space. The camera crew, however, isn't as gracious. They surround the contestants, getting in their faces as much as possible.

"Do you miss this?" asks Jasmine.

I think about the lack of sleep and stress. "Not so much."

Jasmine laughs. "You guys were our guinea pigs. We figured out what worked and what didn't. The current contestants are benefiting from that. Sorry."

I smile. "Tell me about it. I would have killed for a challenge like this!"

"Thank you," pipes up Missy. "All my idea."

Jasmine rolls her eyes. "She's said that so many times, you'd think the *decade* was her idea."

Missy frowns at Jasmine, and the two start bickering. Just like old times. I walk away to chat with Hunter.

"How's Stefan treating you?" he asks.

"Good," I reply. "I'm learning a lot."

"That's the point. We worried a bit about whether the mentoring designers would take our winners seriously."

I think about how to respond to his unasked question. "Stefan and the designers I've worked with have been really supportive. Not everyone feels the same, but overall it's been great."

Hunter pats my shoulder. "Just brush off the rude people. That's what I do."

I nod and look at the clock. Somehow thirty minutes have already passed.

"Let's walk around," Hunter suggests.

We start at one corner, leaving the other for Missy and Jasmine. The first girl I see is wearing a nametag that reads June and is hard at work pinning a long piece of gauzy white material onto her mannequin. She pins fringe to the bottom of the gauze, and I start to envision the skirt she's designing. On the mannequin's bust, June pins paisley material. I remember the elements she selected were gauze and paisley.

I'm not sure why she decided to add fringe, but I give her the benefit of the doubt.

Hunter is about to speak to her when the camera crew suddenly pounces. "Let's get back to her," he says.

The next contestant, Dani, is working barefoot. Her flaming red hair is now tied back with a scrap of fabric.

"Want to tell us about your design?" Hunter asks as we approach.

"Love to!" says Dani. She talks enthusiastically about her black-and-white op-art tank dress, focusing on the swirly pattern she's adding. All the while, she continues working, not taking her eyes off her piece. "I'm going to add sleeves, but I have to figure out what will work. Of course, the sleeves might throw everything out of whack, but what can you do? I'm a fly-by-the-seat-of-your-pants kind of girl."

"I wish I could be more like that," I say. "Good luck."

Our next stop is Kyle, the boy with the rainbow Mohawk. He's frantically pinning and cutting something resembling a micro-mini. Suddenly he starts pacing and muttering about thread and adhesive tape. His sneaker catches on the carpet, and he crashes into his mannequin. It tumbles on top of him, and the cameras are immediately in his face, capturing each gruesome second.

Hunter stops to talk to him, but I give him space. I see Missy has moved on to Carrie, and I go join her.

"What do you think so far?" asks Missy.

"I feel for all of them," I say.

"You can be the softie today," Missy says with a smile. "Speaking of, should we discuss Carrie's, um, creation?"

Missy steps aside, and I see all of Carrie's design. Unfortunately, she didn't stop at the two patterns she picked. The hemp culottes she's working on could have been paired with a turquoise belt or a beaded peace sign. Instead, she's laying it on thick with flower power. The hems are embroidered with flowers, as are the knees and belt. The turquoise peasant blouse has peace signs bordering the sleeves. To tie it all together, Carrie added beading and fringe.

I rack my brain for words of encouragement. "You really went all out," I manage. "What made you go beyond the two patterns you originally chose?"

"The more patterns, the better," Carrie replies, beaming. "I'm also adding beads to the ends of the fringe. Can't hurt, right?"

It's already a disaster. More beading won't matter. I wish I could tell her to start over and stick with just turquoise and peace signs, but guidance isn't allowed. "Do what you think is best," I say, smiling.

"Chloe's too nice," Missy tells Jasmine when we're standing beside her a few minutes later.

Jasmine looks at Carrie's design. "Don't tell me she was optimistic about that monstrosity . . ."

I shift uncomfortably. Carrie's piece *is* a mess, but it still seems unfair to let one bad decision determine everything. "Everyone has a bad day," I mumble, trying to stick up for her.

"She's had a few," says Jasmine. She glances over at the clock — one hour left. Two hours until I see Jake. Taping is sure to be done by then.

"She has promise," Hunter says, joining us. "But not everyone is cut out for these competitions. It's a lot of pressure."

The judges continue examining the designs, and I try to catch up with those I've missed. One piece immediately catches my attention. The designer, Jared, has his long, dark hair pulled back into a ponytail. His mannequin is dressed in a free-flowing, white cotton skirt and a belt embellished with turquoise stones and beads. The top is a nod to the form-fitting clothes of the sixties.

"I like how you incorporated the turquoise as well as the form-fitting element," I tell him.

"I was trying to meld the two styles of the time," says Jared. "There was the group with the tighter, shorter clothing, and then there was the hippie movement. The turquoise stones and beading are a nod to my Native

60s-INSPIRED CONTESTANT *Designs*

BLACK & WHITE COLOR PALETTE

OP-ART SWIRLS

SLEEVELESS MINIDRESS

DANI'S BLACK & WHITE TANK DRESS

teen DESIGN DIVA

American heritage. The culture really influenced fashion in the sixties."

"I'm looking forward to seeing the completed design," I say, moving on. Jared's design is my favorite so far, and his connection to his heritage reminds me of my connection to my grandfather's cowboy style. Gramps was well known in the rodeo world, and his death — months before the *Design Diva* audition — was really hard for me. But thinking of all he accomplished and letting his memory be the inspiration for my designs helped me stand out.

"Thirty minutes!" calls Hunter.

Contestants immediately start scrambling, flinging their materials in all directions. This is the part the cameras love, but I move to a corner and watch everything unfold from there. I focus on a girl with spiky hair who's frantically putting the finishing touches on a fringed vest. If only she'd left it at that. Instead, she's paired the vest with a dress covered in peace signs and flowers.

"Good thing we're letting two go today," says Jasmine as the judges huddle beside me.

"What?" I say, surprised. "I thought you told the contestants one would be eliminated."

"We did," says Missy. "But that's today's twist. Sometimes you have to mix it up. We didn't mean to leave you in the dark."

I think about the twists during my *Design Diva* competition — everything from endless hand sewing to two tasks in one day. I hated being blindsided. And it doesn't feel any better as a judge than it did as a contestant.

"Time!" yells Hunter. Fifteen pairs of eyes stare at us, dying to know their fate.

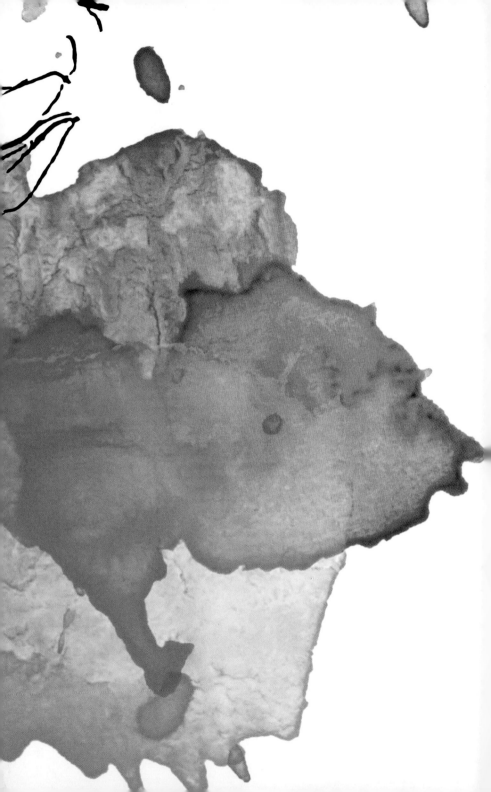

35

I follow Jasmine, Hunter, and Missy to the judges' table and wait for them to take the lead.

"We are so pleased to see such a diverse collection today," Hunter begins. "Your individuality really came through in the challenge."

I nod but then remember that eliminations always start off positive. Then, a judge brings the mood down.

"Unfortunately," Jasmine says, fulfilling my prophecy, "some of you got buried in your unique vision and lost sight of what's fashionable. More is not always better, people."

I see several faces fall and want to say something encouraging, but it's not my turn. Instead, I stay quiet as the judges go from one contestant to the other, giving feedback that's often biting. I do my best to add something supportive.

"Matthew, tell us about your piece, please," Hunter says, calling forward a boy whose design I didn't get a chance to inspect. Seeing it now is a shock. Multiple colors and psychedelic images take over the design. He also added fringe, beading, and stones.

"Sure!" says Matthew. "I wanted a bold design and added several styles and patterns to achieve that. The minidress is modeled after Jackie O's trademark dresses —"

"Sorry, no," Jasmine interrupts. "Mrs. Onassis would have never worn that."

I cringe. Was Jasmine always this mean?

To his credit, Matthew remains unflustered. "Perhaps that's only because such an item wasn't available." He winks, and Jasmine snorts. "Anyway, I wanted to combine Mrs. O's style with the hippie movement."

Missy shifts uncomfortably in her chair. "I'll defer to Chloe on this one."

I swallow. "Hi, Matthew. Well, um, I think you're very brave. You had an idea in your head, and you definitely went with it. Kudos for sticking to your guns," I say diplomatically. I'm not going to crush his dreams.

Matthew falls back into line, and Hunter grins. "Nice work, Chloe," he whispers.

"Thanks," I say, hoping the next contestant is easier.

"Dani, come on down!" Hunter says. As she gets closer, he adds, "The great thing about Dani is that she never fails to surprise us."

Dani smiles. "I do my best."

I look at her finished product, complete with sheer black-and-white sleeves.

"I worried the sleeves might be overkill," Dani says, "but I like how they came out."

"Overkill is definitely not a word that comes to mind here," Missy says. "As usual, you've managed to combine a variety of ideas to create something different. I'm glad you took the risk."

"I agree," I chime in. "The pattern is hypnotizing."

"Well done, Dani," says Hunter. "June, you're up next."

I sit up straighter. When I left June, she still had two patterns to complete.

"I've always loved the flowing skirts of the sixties," June begins. "But I wanted to take it a step further, so I added fringe to the hem. I think it really complements the paisley bodice."

"Hmm," says Jasmine. "I like the color and the pattern, but the fringe doesn't work for me."

"I agree," says Hunter. "You have something really good here, but the fringe takes away from the design."

GEMS &
BEADED
ACCENTS

60s-INSPIRED
CONTESTANT
Designs

PSYCHEDELIC
PATTERN

Beads
+ Gems →

COLORFUL
PATTERN

MATTHEW'S
PSYCHEDELIC
MINIDRESS

June's eyes beg me to say something different, but the truth is, I hate the fringe too. "This design is so promising," I start. "Your color choices work really well, and I love the beading."

"Thank you," June says.

The judges continue with the other contestants. Kyle's design survived his fall, but it's still a mess. His bell-bottom pants have bells at the hems, and the shirt is a combination of polka dots and wavy lines. Pulling it all together is a tie-dyed macramé vest.

When it's my turn, I stick to keeping things positive. "It's a little busy for me, but I admire your ambition," I say.

Jasmine snorts. "Last but not least, we have Jared."

"Like some of my previous designs, I wanted to include my Native American background," Jared says, stepping forward. "My grandfather, who recently passed, was always such a force in my life. He was so proud of our heritage."

Jared chokes up, and a lump forms in my throat too. Just like me, he has a connection to his grandfather. And just like me, he's used it for inspiration.

"Your inspiration clearly shines through," Jasmine says, her voice surprisingly kind. "You've merged two elements of sixties style very successfully."

"I like the addition of the turquoise stones around the collar. The stones and belt really pull the pieces together," I add.

60s-INSPIRED CONTESTANT *Design*

RETRO ACCESSORIES

TIE-DYED MACRAMÉ VEST

Wave + Dot Print Top.

Print Vest

Bell bottoms with actual bells!

KYLE'S BELL-BOTTOM PANTS & PATTERNED BLOUSE

"Thank you," says Jared, his voice sounding stronger now.

"Thank you for all your hard work and creativity," Hunter says. "Now it's time for the judges to deliberate. We'll call you back in when we have a decision."

The contestants leave the room, and Hunter, Missy, Jasmine, and I begin debating the positives and negatives of each design. I glance at the clock. Jake and I are supposed to meet in an hour.

"Wasn't Jared's design the best?" I ask.

"His was fantastic, but there are positives in many of the contestants' designs," Missy tells me. "Besides, we have to let two go, and there were too many problematic designs to make that decision easy."

"I liked Dani's design too," I offer.

"Agreed," Hunter says.

We continue to deliberate and have no trouble placing Dani and Jared into the favorites category. Choosing the bottom designers is tougher.

Without the contestants present, I can speak more freely. "June's fringe was overkill," I say. "But it was just one extra addition. Carrie's and Matthew's designs had more issues. They should have stuck to two styles each."

Jasmine nods appreciatively. "I would have liked to have seen more of this Chloe with the contestants," she says.

I shake my head. "You guys are great, but they expect negative feedback from you. I'd rather be positive. They all tried their best."

Hunter winks at me. "I'm with Chloe. No need to make her into the big, bad meanie."

"What about Kyle?" Missy asks.

"His design had too much happening. But at least it seemed more cohesive than Carrie's and Matthew's," I say.

"I agree," Missy says. "It was better — but barely."

"So we're set?" I say. I look at the clock, feeling anxious. I don't want to flake out on Jake.

"I think so," Hunter says, "but let's recap."

I try to stay focused as they review the positives and negatives of each design. After a half hour, I look at the clock again. I'm supposed to meet Jake in twenty minutes. There's no way I'll make it. I tap my toes.

"You have somewhere to be, Chloe?" asks Jasmine. Her voice is cool. "If you need to leave, go. We'll explain it to the producers — somehow."

"No, it's okay," I say quickly. "I just need to tell someone I'll be late."

I take out my phone to text Jake, but the battery has died. Could this get any worse? Jasmine is still staring at me. I sigh and put on my best happy face. "I'm all yours."

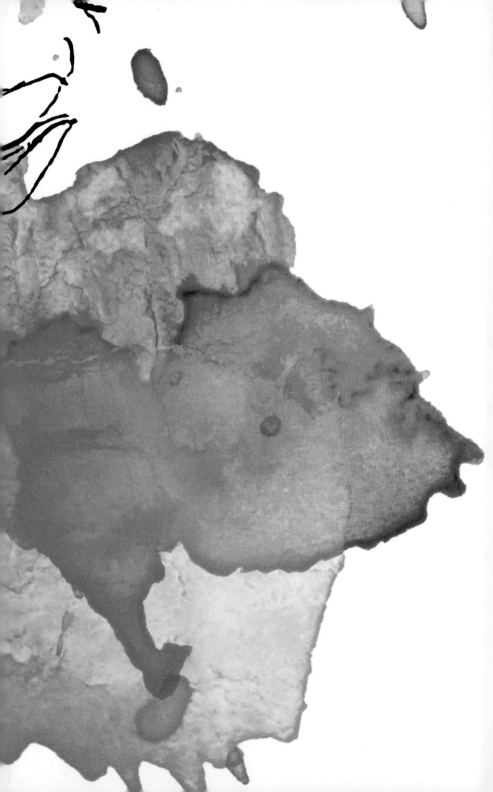

The *Design Diva* deliberations seem to go on forever. By the time the judges announce (unsurprisingly) that Jared is the winner and Carrie and Matthew are eliminated, I've given up all hope of seeing Jake.

Just as I grab my bag to go back to my dorm, Missy says, "Before all our designers leave for the night, I'm sure Chloe wouldn't mind answering any questions you might have."

I put my bag back on my seat and slap on my most encouraging smile. "Of course not." At this point, there's no meeting with Jake, anyway.

Hunter, Missy, and Jasmine gather the contestants and arrange chairs in a circle. Dani raises her hand first. "Which of the designs you did on the show was your favorite?" she asks.

"Definitely the one for the Toys 'R' Us challenge. I was feeling down and not sure how to make something out of the box." The contestants laugh at this and nod, relating to it. "But then I thought about how to make the piece my own. The local fair back in my hometown was a big inspiration for me when I designed my cotton candy-inspired skirt for that challenge."

"How did you sew without machines?" asks June.

"Very stressfully," I say, and everyone laughs again.

"Tell us about your internship," Kyle says.

"It's been amazing," I say. "Stefan Meyers lets me be very hands-on. If you guys think the competition is getting too hard, just think of the internship. It's worth it."

"Are there any mean girls?" asks June. "Like Nina LeFleur from your season?"

I think of Madison and frame my answer carefully. "There will always be people who try to get the best of you. The key is to keep believing in yourself."

I know my answer sounded too perfect, but it's true. Besides, the cameras are still rolling. I don't want my words to be edited into something vicious.

"What do you like best about your internship?" asks Jared.

"Learning new things," I say. "Going into this competition, I thought I had a good handle on fashion design. Even more so after winning. But working for Stefan Meyers has made me realize that there's so much more to learn. I want my own label one day, and there's a lot to know about running it."

I'm starting to feel more at ease and less anxious when someone calls out, "Whatever happened with you and that cute boy?"

I blush. Jake gave me a big hug onstage after I won, and the cameras panned to him during the last challenge, so it's not surprising the contestants remember him. "Um, we're still friends," I say. *Hopefully*, I want to add. I imagine Jake waiting for me, trying to call me, and then walking back to his apartment — alone. It makes me sad.

I steer the conversation elsewhere. "What do you wish would be different about the competition?" I ask. I wish someone had asked this during my season.

"More sleep would be nice," says Jared.

"A little more time to start our designs before everyone swarms in," says Kyle.

I nod. I can appreciate that. I spend a few more minutes chatting before wrapping things up. I give the new crop of designers my e-mail in case they have more questions.

"Stay in touch," Jasmine tells me. "We're rooting for you out there."

I hug the judges goodbye and walk back to my dorm. It was a great day, but I wonder if I could have done things differently. Should I have left? What would have happened if I had? I unlock the door to my suite, wanting to charge my phone and be alone, but Bailey is sitting in the common room.

"Hey," I say as I plug in my phone.

She puts down her sketch. "What's wrong? You look like you're going to cry. Oh! Before I forget, Jake was here looking for you. Did he find you?"

I look at her miserably and tell her the whole story.

"Ugh. That stinks," Bailey says when I finish.

"I know. And I feel so ungrateful. I got to be a *Design Diva* judge, which was amazing, but I really wanted to see Jake." I shake my head. "I should have left."

Bailey stares at me like I've lost my mind. "Are you insane? You did *not* just say that, Chloe. This is your dream we're talking about! I know you're still in high school, but fashion design is all about opportunities and catching a break. Talent too, but there are a lot of talented designers out there. You don't just throw away an opportunity like that!"

I've never seen Bailey annoyed at me, but she clearly is now. "Sorry," I mumble.

Bailey sighs. "I don't mean to lecture you, but so many people would kill for what you have. I mean, if someone told you last year to walk a mile in a pair of Manolo Blahniks for this chance, wouldn't you have done it?"

I nod. Miles. Marathons. Anything. My phone buzzes, signaling that it finally has some juice, and I see six texts from Jake, all asking where I am. The last one says, "Guess you're busy. Hope you're okay."

I immediately call Jake's cell, but it goes straight to voicemail. I leave a message saying how sorry I am and explaining what happened.

When I put the phone down, Bailey does the same with her sketchpad. "If it's meant to be, he'll understand. Get some sleep. You'll feel better in the morning."

I swallow, feeling a pit in my stomach. "Thanks for listening."

"Any time."

I start to go into my room when Bailey says, "Chloe?"

I turn around.

"You're really talented. Don't let anything stand in your way."

I nod. "Thanks again."

I get ready for bed and try to focus on all the positives ahead of me. All the things I've always wanted. Based on what Michael said, I've barely experienced PR. That's to happen in the days to come. I close my eyes and imagine Fashion Week, runways, models, and my designs. I imagine Stefan saying how lucky he is to have such a fabulous intern. I keep these images in my head and don't let them get away.

Dear Diary,

Where has the time gone? I can't believe I only have two weeks left in New York City. I'm really going to miss my dorm at FIT and my suitemates. Well . . . most of them. Bailey and Avery are terrific, but Madison still makes rude comments whenever she can. No matter what I do, she still acts like I don't deserve to be here. Luckily, the head designers I've worked with at Stefan Meyers don't feel the same way.

Interning has been a balancing act for sure — especially working in different departments at the same time — but I've learned so much in the six weeks I've been at Stefan Meyers. This next week is all about getting everything ready for Fashion Week! I'm still in PR with Michael, plus I'll be helping Laura, Taylor, and the sound engineer. Stefan also mentioned the chance to work with models, but he hasn't figured out the day yet.

Juggling everything has been a lot harder than I thought it would be. Especially when it comes to my social life. Don't get me wrong. I didn't think I'd spend my internship just hanging out, but I thought I'd have more time to sketch and see Jake, especially since he's in school here. Instead, I've spent my days running from one department to the

to the next, working late, and falling into bed exhausted at night.

As for Jake? I'm just hoping we're still friends. I still haven't talked to him since I stood him up a few days ago. It's not like I *wanted* to blow him off — but I couldn't exactly walk out on being a guest judge on *Teen Design Diva*. It just stinks. I know how lucky I am to have all these great opportunities, but I can't help feeling bad for hurting Jake.

On the bright side, my best friend Alex is coming to visit! She's only staying for the weekend, but at least it's something. I wish she could be here during Fashion Week too, but maybe it's for the best. The balancing act I was talking about before is sure to get a lot harder in the next two weeks, and if Alex were here during Stefan's show, I'd feel bad about not spending time with her.

I can't believe I get to be a part of Fashion Week! It's literally a dream come true. Stefan says these next two weeks "are the ones that really matter." I'm sure it will be stressful but exciting too. And to think, I've been there from start to finish.

Xoxo — Chloe

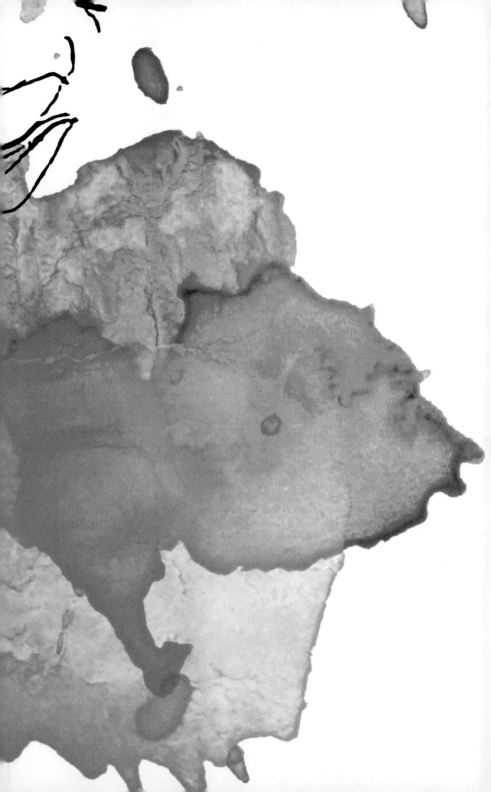

37

As I get dressed for work Monday morning, I try to focus on the positive. I feel ridiculous focusing on the fact that Jake and I still haven't spoken after I accidentally blew him off.

As if he read my mind, my phone buzzes with a text from Jake. "Meet for lunch to talk?"

"Definitely!" I write back. Hopefully that means he's not too mad at me.

Now that I know I have lunch plans, I go to my closet to find the perfect outfit. Today's answer comes in a graphic midi skirt in black and white, a short-sleeved black blouse, and black, multi-strap, chunky-heeled sandals. I put on my makeup, do a final once-over in front of the mirror, and am ready to take on whatever the day brings.

When I arrive at the office, Michael is waiting for me. "How goes the celebrity life?" he asks.

"Please," I say with a laugh. "It's hardly that."

"The *Design Diva* website begs to differ," he says, showing me the site on his laptop.

I glance at it and see a photo of me with a caption that says, "Meet the Surprise *Teen Design Diva* Judge." I stifle a groan. Great. That's all I need. When I first started here, Madison and some of her friends called me Diva Girl, like I was some TV star with no talent. Now it's sure to start up again. I don't want anyone thinking fame is all I want.

"Don't look so glum," says Michael. "This news puts Stefan in the spotlight even more. He was right about you judging the show. It was great publicity for the label."

"It *was* a great experience," I agree. "But I'm not running to Hollywood just yet. I'm here to serve." I perform a mock bow.

"Good to hear, because we have a lot to do," says Michael.

Just then, my phone buzzes, and I do my best to keep my focus on my boss.

"We need to get gift bags ready for Fashion Week," Michael continues. "I have the items in bins here —"

My phone buzzes again, and this time I sneak a peek. It's Jake with a meeting place for lunch.

"Chloe?" says Michael, an edge to his voice.

I snap back to attention. "Sorry," I say sheepishly.

Michael sighs. "As I was saying, the items are in the bins, and the bags are here. Everyone will receive an iPhone cover, but the women's bags will also contain this perfume and the men's will get this cologne."

My phone buzzes again, and I can't help but look.

"Is that your paparazzi calling?" Michael asks. He's smiling but clearly annoyed. "Do you want me to leave you alone so you can talk?"

I turn off my phone. "No, sorry."

"Do you have any questions?" Michael asks.

"I got it," I say, repeating all his instructions to show that I was listening.

"Very well. I'll check in after lunch." With that, he turns and walks back to his office.

For the first time, I really take in the bins before me. There's a lot of stuff. Forcing myself to stay on task, I crouch down on the floor and start putting the bags together. I inspect the perfumes, wondering if the fragrances would work well on me. After about fifty bags, though, my mind starts to wander, and I don't care about the colors or perfume smells. I just go through the motions.

After a while I get up to stretch and check the clock. Only an hour to go until I'm supposed to meet Jake. I hear Michael's door opening and glance at the bags before me. I feel proud of how many I've assembled until I see the bins with cologne — they're still completely full.

I panic and check the gift bags. No! I put the same things in all of them. *This is what happens when you don't pay attention, Chloe*, I chide myself. I quickly empty out the bags and start fixing my mistake. Thankfully, Michael's door is closed again. For the next hour, I keep my head in the game, feeling lucky I caught my mistake in time.

* * *

When I get to the café Jake suggested, I shield my eyes and scan the crowd for his face.

"Table for one?" asks a waitress.

"Um, no, I'm waiting —" I begin. Suddenly, I hear my name.

"Over here, Chloe!" Jake calls, waving his arm in the air. He's already seated at a small table, and I walk over to join him, smoothing my skirt as I take a seat.

"You look nice," he says.

"Thanks," I say, taking a nervous sip of water. "So, um, about last week . . ."

Jake takes my hand, and butterflies immediately appear in my stomach. "I was annoyed because I wanted to see you, but I know it wasn't your fault."

"It was," I say. "I should have texted you sooner — as soon as the judging thing came up. I'm really sorry.

Everything has just been nuts. And with Fashion Week around the corner it's only going to get crazier."

"You're right about that," Jake agrees. "You'll have to be on hand whenever they need you."

I think about this as the waitress takes our orders. I order a muffin and tea — I don't think I can eat much more. What Jake said is true. If we had little time to see each other before, there will be even less time now. I can't spend the next two weeks being tied to my texts.

"The timing hasn't been great for us, has it?" Jake says.

I smile sadly. I know he's thinking the same thing I am. "At least we'll always have California, right?"

Jake grins. "Definitely. I'll be on the lookout for your Fashion Week designs. And I visit my dad in California a lot. We can always hang then."

Maybe romance isn't in the cards now, but I realize I've made a good friend. When you're following your dreams, that's a must.

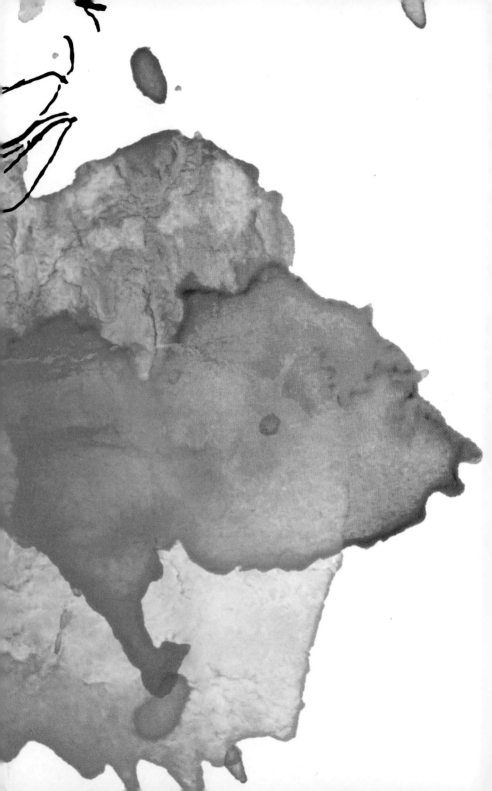

When I get back to the office, I see several neatly stacked piles of papers waiting for me on my desk.

"I've looked through the gift bags, and they're a go. Nice job," Michael says, walking over. "The next task requires more brain power."

"Sign me up," I say.

"It's crucial we get information about Stefan's designs out to the public," Michael explains. "I need you to call the newspapers and television networks that have agreed to interview Stefan to confirm time, place, etcetera. You'd be surprised how often the details get mixed up. We can't afford for that to happen."

Michael grabs a paper from the top of the stack and hands it to me — a list of contacts. I glance at the names and recognize some of them from television and red carpet shows. My mouth goes dry just thinking about calling them.

"What will I say?" I ask.

"I have that ready for you. Just follow this script," Michael says, handing me another piece of paper. "The schedule of events is here as well."

I relax a little. What could be easier than reading off a paper?

"Lastly," Michael continues, "I've compiled a list of fashion bloggers and journalists for you to touch base with. We want to make sure they're at the show, viewing Stefan's designs. Again, everything has been arranged, but confirmation is key. We don't want to miss these opportunities."

Michael hands me another template to follow with all the information explained. "You can do these confirmations via email. Just copy and paste the contents of this paper, changing the names as necessary. I've emailed it to you as well."

"No problem," I say, trying to sound confident.

Once Michael leaves, I try to get down to business, but my insecurities take over. During this internship, I've proven time and time again that I can tackle new challenges. But apparently worrying each time a new one surfaces never ends.

I give myself five minutes of freak-out time, letting all the worst-case scenarios run through my head. I could flub the script and say the wrong day. I could read the wrong template. I could totally forget to call someone on the list. Someone could be rude and hang up on me.

But the more I think about the worst possibilities, the more ridiculous they seem. I mean, why would someone hang up on me? *Focus, Chloe,* I think, pushing all the craziness out of my mind.

Taking a deep breath, I make my way down the list of contacts I need to call. For each one, I follow Michael's script and consult the schedule, making sure to get all the details right. With each call, my voice is more assertive.

The only downside, which is probably something I should have figured out earlier, is that I don't actually get to talk to any of the famous people on the list. An assistant — or maybe even an intern just like me — answers every call. Which, duh, makes total sense. Glamorous people are probably busy doing glamorous things.

Once I've confirmed all Stefan's interview dates and times, I move on to the next project. Writing emails to the bloggers and journalists is far less nerve-racking, because I don't have to worry about what to say.

I work the entire afternoon but manage to finish all confirmations. For both the calls and e-mails, I make sure to keep careful records of everyone I contacted and everyone who's replied. I roll my neck from side to side and double-check my lists to make sure I left nothing out.

"Well done," says Michael when I show him my completed work. "I know Stefan promised you PR would be all about glitz and glamour, but what you've been doing is so important for the show's success. I really appreciate it."

It would have been cool to talk with someone famous, but being so involved in the process was rewarding on its own as well. And knowing that I played even a small part in a glossy print ad or *Entertainment Tonight* interview is still pretty amazing.

"Today was great. I'm just glad to be involved!" I say.

Michael's eyes twinkle. "Fabulous! Tomorrow, though, be prepared for a little glam."

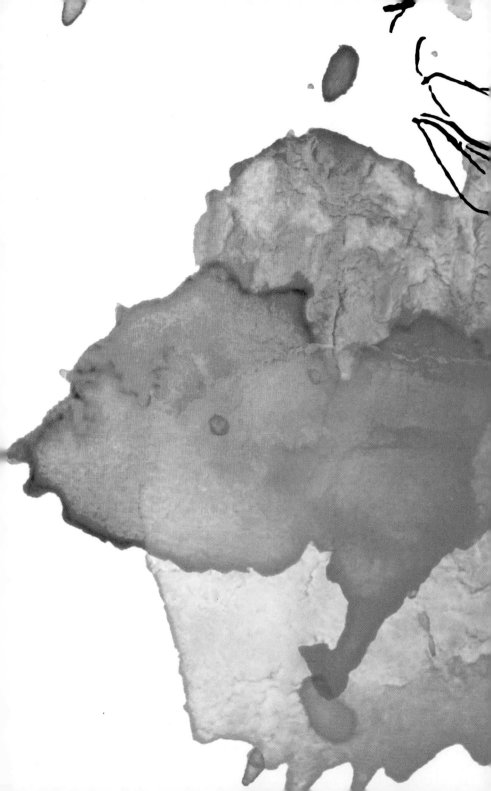

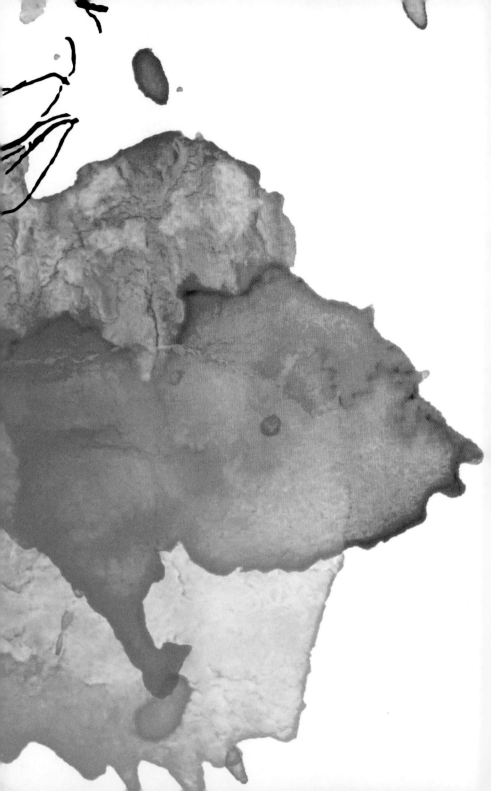

Tuesday morning, I'm up extra early. Michael didn't want to reveal what was on the agenda for today in case there was a last-minute change, so I'm not sure what to dress for. After several closet scans, I leave the dorm in a pair of coated brown jeans, a white blouse, gold cuff bracelet, and metallic sandals. I'm too excited to sit still on the subway, so I walk to the office, doing my best not to run.

When I get to Michael's office, he's not alone — Laura and Taylor, the head designers I've worked with, and Liesel McKay are there too. Liesel is an amazing designer in her own right, but she's also Jake's mom and my mentor from my *Teen Design Diva* days.

What are they doing here? I wonder. *I'm not supposed to see them until Thursday. Did I do something wrong? And if so, what does Liesel have to do with that? Is she here to soften the blow?*

Thankfully, Michael immediately puts me at ease. "Chloe, I'm glad you're here. We're doing a dry run of next week's runway show. We'll be working with the models and doing any last-minute alterations. We also need to finalize the order in which the pieces will appear. The photographers will take pictures so we can have a visual to use the day of. I need you to help with whatever they need."

I breathe a sigh of relief. Why do I always jump to the worst conclusions? Having Laura and Taylor here makes total sense. Laura's knits and the art deco designs she did with Taylor will be showcased during Fashion Week. And Liesel and Taylor were working on a project for Fashion Week too.

"When do we start?" I ask.

"About twenty minutes," says Michael. "We have a studio on the eleventh floor, and they're still setting it up. Get yourself some coffee — relax if you can."

Coffee will energize me more, but it will give me something to do. Besides, I can't risk not being fully awake!

* * *

Twenty minutes later, fully caffeinated, I follow Michael, Laura, Taylor, and Liesel upstairs to the studio. There are white sheets covering the floor and lights set up all around the room. A group of photographers is standing off to one side. As soon as we walk in, one of them walks over and extends his hand. "Jordan LeMure," he introduces himself.

I know that name! He's been interviewed on a bunch of fashion shows. "Chloe Montgomery," I say.

He smiles. "I've seen your work. That was some good television!"

I blush. "Thanks."

Just then, Laura calls out, "The models are here! Chloe, can you help get them lined up in the hall?"

"Watch for my cues to bring the models in," Jordan says before I leave. "Laura, Taylor, and Liesel will tell you which pieces each girl should be wearing."

"Got it," I say, rushing into the hallway to meet the models.

Laura hands me a list with the outfits the models will be trying on. "They will be modeling the clothes in this order," she says. "You can find all the needed items on this rack." She motions to a stand a few feet away.

The models slip into sky-high heels and line up, knowing the drill better than I do. I scan the checklist Laura gave me and pull down a short-sleeved, gray wool dress with an art deco-inspired skirt. I like the way the black and white pleating spices up the gray.

While that model is dressing, I pull down more clothes so there is minimal lag between shoots. I expect the models to give me attitude since I'm younger than them and clearly new to this, but they just smile, take the clothes, and say thank you.

As beautiful as the clothing is, it's amazing how the models make the clothing come alive. The gray wool dress, for example, is stylish on its own. However, the model's long torso draws my attention to the stretch of the fabric. When she walks, my eyes are pulled to the belt at the waist and the geometric pattern of the skirt. She stops in the center of the floor, allowing the photographers to take photos.

The next dress on my list is one I remember discussing with Laura. It's a white sleeveless tank dress with blue accents and a pleated white-and-blue skirt. A model tries it on and walks toward the photographers. Her walk has a bounce to it, showing she gets the fun, flirty intent of the piece.

"One minute," I hear Jordan saying as the model finishes her shoot. "Chloe, come here, please."

I look at him like he's made a mistake, but he motions me over. "I need you to stand in for the model while we fix the lighting. Can you do that?"

"Just stand?" I ask.

"Move around a little too," Jordan says. He has me walk a few paces while the other photographers play with the lighting and check their lenses. Seeing what I have of the models, I know I'm nowhere near their level, but for these few minutes, I feel glamorous anyway.

When I'm done, I rush back to the racks and continue passing out clothes. There are two dresses left in Laura's collection before we break for lunch. I pull a short-sleeved V-neck sweater dress off the rack. The cream-colored pleated skirt pairs well with the top, which is an array of converging black, white, and gold lines.

The last piece is the lavender dress with black trim Laura designed. I'm filled with happiness as I remember her telling me that my pocket design was her inspiration for this piece. The model slips it on, and I grin as I watch the garment come to life.

As we break for lunch, the models change out of their heels and back into the flats they were wearing when they arrived. I remember the day I walked to the *Vogue* offices, feet full of blisters. My heels weren't nearly as tall as the ones these models are wearing. Their feet have to be killing them, but you wouldn't know it. They didn't complain when Jordan asked for photo retakes or had them stand perfectly still under the hot lights. It's all about making Stefan's styles a success. I need to remember that the next time I consider complaining.

GRAY WOOL DRESS

SM FASHION WEEK Designs

SWEATER DRESS

ART DECO PRINT

TANK DRESS

GOLD LINE ACCENTS

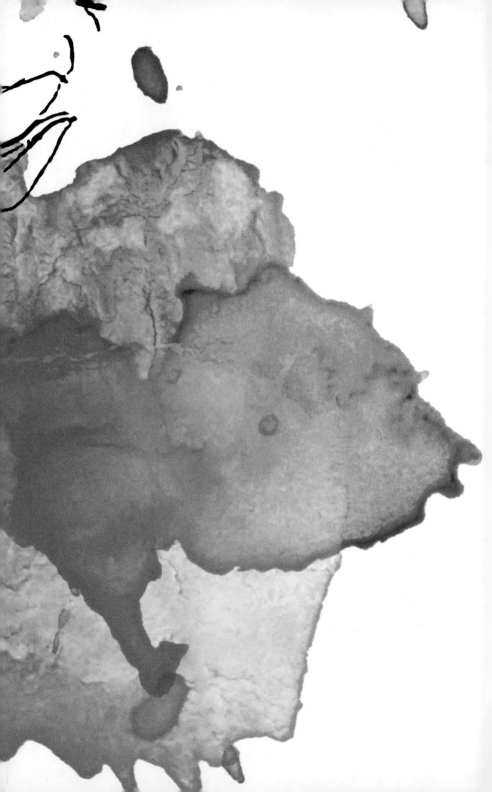

When I get back to my dorm that night, Madison, Bailey, Avery, and I chomp on Chinese food and talk Fashion Week. "I can't wait for you guys to meet Alex on Saturday," I say. "I'm so excited for her to get here!"

"Oh, that's right," says Madison, frowning. "I forgot she was coming."

Avery waves her hand dismissively in Madison's direction. "The more the merrier. When we hang in my dorm back at school, we can cram twenty people in there to watch a movie."

"She'd better not be bringing an entourage with her," Madison grumbles.

"Just her," I say, then try to change the subject. "I wish she could help out with Fashion Week. I got to work with some of the models today! It was so cool!"

"I could never model," says Avery. "I'm way too shy for that."

"I'm sooo not graceful," Bailey adds. "I'd probably trip on the catwalk and ruin the designs."

I laugh. "Me too! But I got to stand in for one of the models today — just for a second — and I'll admit, it was pretty cool. Intimidating, but cool."

"I'd rather see my name in lights for my designs, not for how I appear in front of a camera," Madison says snidely.

You'd have to be an idiot not to get that dig. I take a deep breath and remind myself that my stint on *Teen Design Diva* was not about fame — it was about my skill as a designer.

"Agreed," I say. "But if it weren't for models, the designs wouldn't get noticed."

Madison turns away from me and directs her question to Avery and Bailey. "Do you think we'll get to be involved in the show?"

"My cousin interned out in LA a while back and got to help out with Fashion Week there. She mostly ran around making sure all the set-up went smoothly. But she said she got to help in the back of the house getting clothing ready, dressing the models, that sort of thing too. We won't see our names in lights yet, but all this stuff is also really important."

Madison frowns. "I guess," she says, sounding unimpressed. "I was hoping to talk to celebs or something. I worked really hard in the jewelry department, *and* I helped with dresses." She turns to me. "Don't you want everyone to know which pieces you put together or which design is yours?"

I'm so surprised she's talking to me again that it takes me a minute to answer. I'm sure she's expecting me to rant about wanting all the credit I can get, and I'd be lying if I said I didn't care about that at least a little. But one thing I've learned the past six weeks is that it takes a lot of people to put something together. There are plenty of designers who've been working a lot longer than I have who deserve credit too. All our ideas together, bouncing off each other, blending into one, is what made each design work.

I open my mouth to answer, but it's obvious I took too long, because Madison rolls her eyes and says, "Oh, please. Don't even try to say you don't care about that. Everyone does!"

"Why are you always so mad?" Bailey asks Madison.

"I just think we all have to pay our dues," Madison says, giving me a pointed look. "I work hard too, and no one's said a word about what I've come up with!"

"That doesn't mean they haven't noticed," I say quietly. "The only reason —"

"Whatever," Madison interrupts. "I don't need advice from Miss Diva here." She picks up the remains of her food, throws it in the trash, and slams the door to her room.

"Oh my gosh," says Avery. "That girl is a bottomless pit of negativity. What is her problem?"

I shake my head. "Who knows? I mean, to a certain extent, I get where she's coming from. We all want the spotlight. Waiting for it to happen can be hard."

Bailey nods. "That's true, I suppose. But it still doesn't give her the right to be so rude."

Avery, Bailey, and I finish eating and spend the rest of the night chatting and gossiping, imagining the day, years from now, when interns will be working for us.

* * *

The next morning, I'm putting the finishing touches on my outfit — a short-sleeved, black triangle dress — when my phone buzzes with a text from Michael: "Meet me at Lincoln Center."

I quickly pull my hair back with a metallic clip, grab my sketchpad, and run out the door. I'm looking forward to the twenty-minute subway ride. I haven't had nearly

enough time during my internship to work on my own designs, but there's nothing like Fashion Week to inspire!

When the train arrives, I plop down in the nearest open seat and take out my sketchpad. So far most of my sketches have been of people I've seen around the city. Today, I'm thinking of some Chloe Montgomery originals. I choose a shimmery blue pencil and sketch a high-low dress that swoops to the ankles in the back and stops just above the knee at the front. I play with the idea of straps but nix them in favor of a halter neckline and keyhole opening at the bust. Suddenly, I get another idea. This could be the perfect dress for prom — my own personal version of Fashion Week!

We arrive at my stop before I know it, and I stow my sketchbook, mentally vowing to return to my design later. I hurry off the train and into Lincoln Center, where I quickly spot Michael waiting for me.

"Today we're scouting out our Fashion Week location!" he announces, sounding energized and excited. "Since Stefan's emphasis is on art deco, we want a clean, white tent. Anything too over-the-top will distract from the designs."

Michael cups his hands around his eyes like he's going to take a picture and steps back, trying to visualize the area from all angles. "This," he says, motioning to the sides, "is where the audience will sit. The runway will flow down the middle."

I picture what he's describing — models walking down the runway, an opening at the back of the runway from which they'll enter, chairs on either side, everything in white, maybe little white lights on the ceiling.

"It needs something," says Michael. "Like a centerpiece of some kind."

I play the show in my mind. Models wearing Taylor and Liesel's art deco designs strut down the runway. One is wearing a satin gown embroidered with overlapping V's. Another showcases a floor-length gown of shimmering silver satin. Dresses with light beading and fringe with metallic threading parade in my head. I remember the press release I worked on with Michael — "Stefan Meyers Brings Back Roaring Twenties with Elegant Art Deco." Whatever we add has to be grand but not take away from the designs.

"How about an enormous chandelier at the end of the runway?" I suggest, imagining light ricocheting off the crystals and illuminating the metallic threading on the dresses. "That would really add some drama and glamour. We could do something reminiscent of the 1920s."

Michael closes his eyes. "That will be perfect! The bee's knees, some might say! Just like you, my dear."

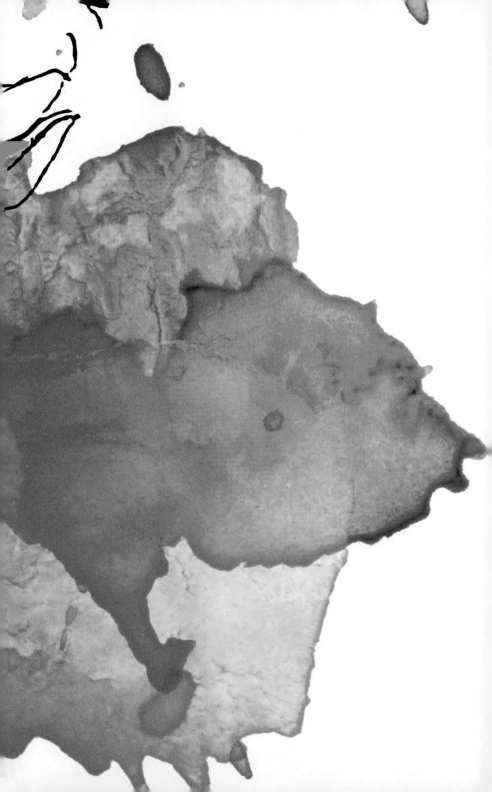

On Thursday I'm back with Laura and Taylor. As soon as I arrive, they wheel out racks of clothes that will be used in next week's show. I saw some of the designs during the model fitting, but things were moving so quickly, I didn't pay attention to every garment. Now I take a closer look and am thrilled to see some items I worked on during my internship.

"The show is Wednesday, so we're down to the wire," says Laura. "We'll need your help getting these ready and packaged away. Everything needs to be steamed."

Taylor wheels out a machine and tells me the dos and don'ts — mainly how not to burn myself or ruin the clothes. Then she fills the machine with water and runs the handheld attachment over the garments. All wrinkles disappear.

"Practice on these first," Taylor says, pointing to a pile of clothes.

I pick up the steamer and slowly go over the clothes. The water drips on a few of the pieces, but after a couple tries I get the hang of it.

"There are forty pieces here," says Laura. "Take your time. If you need us, we're only a shout away."

They leave, and I do a few more practice steaming runs before moving on to the Fashion Week items. Steaming may not be glamorous, but it's surprisingly relaxing. It's also really gratifying watching tiny wrinkles disappear and seeing the clothes come out looking like new.

I spot the flowered pockets and denim designs, along with the art deco sweater dress I worked on with Laura. I remember discussing how great the dress would look with a geometric pattern and metallic threading. Seeing the finished piece is like a dream come true.

The silk dresses I worked on with Taylor are there too, and I remember the sketches I drew for her. I find the dressy jackets I helped Laura design and hold them up to the dresses. The shawl collars in silk and velvet complement Taylor's floor-length gowns. Another jacket, lightly embroidered with pearls, helps bring out the pearl embellishments on one of Taylor's art deco dresses.

I smile to myself as I steam. There won't be a place in the program that says, "Chloe helped with these," but I'll know. And for now, that's enough.

* * *

After lunch, Laura and Taylor examine my work.

"Nice job," says Laura. "My first time steaming I ruined five dresses."

"I only ruined two," Taylor brags.

Laura shoots her a knowing look. "I wouldn't get cocky. If I remember correctly, most of the stuff you steamed was dripping wet. It took days to salvage it."

Taylor scowls. "Maybe. But it *was* salvaged."

"Barely," Laura mumbles.

I stare at them. Their competitiveness kind of reminds me of the rivalry I have with Nina LeFleur, a girl from back home. The only difference is that Laura and Taylor seem to like each other too. "Where do I go next?" I ask, trying to diffuse the argument.

Taylor checks her watch. "Stefan wants you to see what sound editing is all about. Gary, the sound engineer, is the brains behind the music for Fashion Week."

"His studio is on the ninth floor," says Laura. "I'll take you there."

When we arrive on the ninth floor, a guy wearing a white button-down over dark blue jeans greets us. "I'm Gary," he says, tipping his black derby hat.

"Chloe," I say, extending my hand.

"Take good care of her," Laura says before heading off.

"I'm working on the music the models will be walking to," Gary explains as we head to his studio. "I'm thinking something fun and dance-centric." He plays a few samples and has me walk to the music. I feel a little silly and wonder if he's making fun of me, but when I peek at his face, I see that he's deep in concentration, fidgeting with the dials and changing the speed and songs.

To be honest, I don't usually pay attention to the songs used on the runway. All I focus on are the designs. It makes me wish Alex were already here — music is so her thing.

Gary plays with the dials, switches tunes, and writes something down. He does this a few more times before taking a break. "What do you think?" he asks.

I'm not a music expert, but I like the beat. "The rhythm is good," I offer.

Gary nods. "Good. I think so too," he says.

"Do you like being behind the scenes like this?" I ask. As soon as the words are out, I put my hand over my mouth. That sounded kind of rude.

Thankfully, Gary just smiles. "You mean not getting the spotlight?" He shrugs. "It bugged me when I started out. Reviewers rarely, if ever, mention the songs. But it's cool. I've been doing this for years now, and I love watching the impact the right songs have on the show."

He has a point, I realize. I might not have noticed the songs in the past, but I imagine a fashion show without music — it would be dead and boring.

"I work for a variety of designers and do films too," Gary continues, "but there's something about Fashion Week. There's nothing like that immediate thrill of watching an audience react to the shows. Yeah, it's totally about the designs, but I sometimes see people tapping their feet to the music. It reminds me how important this job is."

I nod. I'm glad Stefan had me spend the afternoon here. It's a perfect reminder of how much goes into a successful fashion show — every step, no matter how small, counts.

Gary and I spend the rest of the day listening to music and testing out songs. By the end of the day, he has a selection ready to go.

"Wow," I say as he packs up, "that's a lot of work for a show that's only fifteen minutes long."

Gary smiles. "You remember that next week. Not everyone wants the spotlight, Chloe. You can have credit without lights shining on your face."

SWEATER
DRESS

PEARL
DETAILS

FLOWER
POCKET
JEANS

METALLIC
THREAD

BIAS-CUT
SILK DRESS

Art Deco-
Inspired
SM Designs

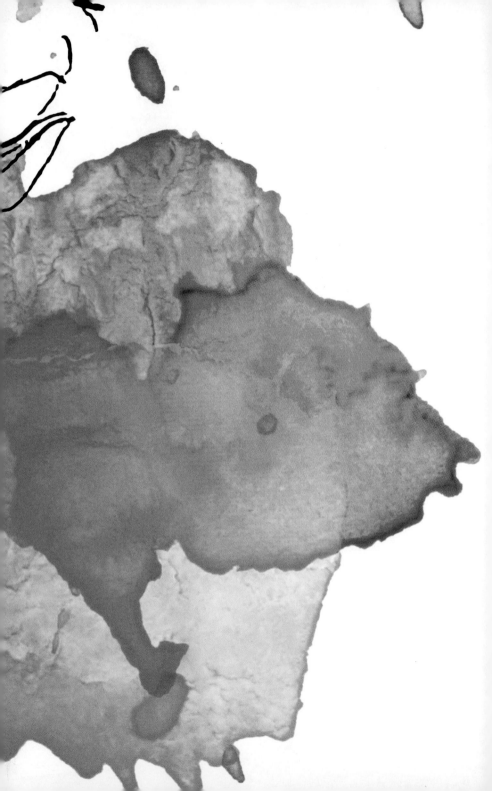

When the weekend finally arrives, I wait impatiently for Alex. Her last text, "Leaving airport now!" was an hour ago. How far is the airport, anyway? Darn New York traffic.

When the taxi finally pulls up in front of my dorm, I rush out to meet it. It's been two months since I've seen Alex, and I miss my best friend so much. She clearly feels the same way, because she already has one foot out the door before the cab has even come to a complete stop.

We throw our arms around each other as we jump and screech. The taxi driver honks his horn and reminds Alex to pay him. "Oops," she says, quickly handing him a wad of cash. Then we get back to yelling and hugging.

I take a step back and see how much Alex has changed. "What happened?" I say, noticing her highlights, makeup, and new outfit — a fitted black T-shirt, distressed boyfriend jeans, and studded black flats. She still looks like the same old Alex, just a much chicer version.

Alex grins and twirls. "You can't have a best friend living the high life and not have that rub off on you. I've been reading fashion blogs and trying to find stuff that is stylish but still feels like me. I wanted to surprise you. You like?"

"Definitely," I say. "Does this mean we can shop together now?" My eyes glaze over as I envision hours of store hopping with Alex. "We have years to make up for!"

"Hold up," says Alex, grimacing a little. "Baby steps. You're making me want to crawl back into sweats."

"Please, no!" I say in mock horror. "Not that!"

Alex laughs, and it reminds me again how happy I am to have my friend here. I wish she could stay longer so I could really show her around NYC, but two days is better than nothing. We quickly take her suitcase up to my room and head over to Bryant Park.

"How do you deal with all these people?" Alex asks as we get jostled on the busy streets.

I shrug. "It doesn't bother me anymore. I actually love it. I'm afraid Santa Cruz's silence will kill me when I get back."

"Don't worry," says Alex, putting her arm around me. "I'll stand outside your window and bang drums all night to make the transition easier."

"Ha! Speaking of home, what have I missed?" I ask. Since I started my internship, there hasn't been much time to gossip with Alex. There's so much I want to talk about. None of it is earth-shattering, but when you're talking to your best friend, it feels like everything is.

Alex fills me in on Nina and her groupies. Turns out Nina has less of an entourage than she did when I left. Apparently, after watching us on *Teen Design Diva*, there's a bit of a divide between Team Nina and Team Chloe.

"I kid you not," Alex says when I look at her in disbelief. "Be prepared to have your own groupies upon your return."

"Just what I need," I say, rolling my eyes. But then I get an idea on how to make good with this ridiculous news. "Maybe they'd want to learn designing and all that. Then they can do it themselves and lay off the hero worship."

"Good luck with that," Alex says as we walk into the park. We sit in the games section and choose a table with Jenga. "So, tell me what's going on with Jake. You've hardly said a word about him lately."

"I figured it would be easier to talk to you about it in person," I say, pulling a wooden piece from the Jenga tower. "He's a really nice guy, and he's so cute, but I have so much going on right now. It's been almost impossible to make time for him. And then when we did make plans, I'd have to cancel. The day of *Teen Design Diva* judging was the worst.

My phone died, so I couldn't tell him I was running late." I frown, still feeling bad about that day.

Alex smiles sympathetically. "That must have been hard for both of you." She pulls a wooden block, and the tower wobbles but doesn't fall.

I nod. "It was. Trying to hang out was too much pressure."

"I'm sorry," says Alex. "I know you really liked him."

"I still do, but it's not like I won't see him again. Besides, boyfriends are drama. Friends always stay." I gently push a loose block from the bottom and stack it beside Alex's piece.

Alex blushes and fiddles with the tab on her soda. "So, um, boyfriends can be drama, but I sort of have one. His name is Dan," she says.

I'm so surprised by her announcement that I almost knock over the blocks. "Why didn't you tell me?"

"It wasn't official until last week, and then I figured I might as well wait and tell you in person," she says. "Are you upset, since you and Jake . . ." Her voice trails off.

I roll my eyes. "Oh my gosh! I told you, I'm fine. Really. Now spill."

"Well," Alex says, pulling a block and causing the tower to wobble, "he likes basketball, just like me. And we've gone hiking a lot."

"Do you make him watch bad reality television with you?" I ask jokingly. I pull a block, and the tower tumbles to the table.

"Nah, that's *our* special thing," Alex says, pointing at me. "But we do scarf Doritos and pizza together."

I laugh. "A match made in heaven. I'm really happy for you."

Alex and I wander around a bit more, even acting silly and riding the carousel. It's mostly full of kids, but people smile at us as we park ourselves on a horse and zebra. We grin as the animals go up and down. Being chic intern Chloe has been great, but I've missed being goofy with Alex.

"Two days is not enough to spend with you at all!" I say as we head back to my dorm. "I wish you could stay and help with Fashion Week."

Alex grins mischievously. "Well . . . that's actually something I've been wanting to talk to you about. I did some research, and I think there might be a way I can stay longer . . ."

* * *

We hurry back to the dorm to run Alex's plan by Avery and Bailey. I'm less excited, however, to see the look on Madison's face when I suggest Alex might stay longer.

"Guys," I say as we walk in, "this is my best friend, Alex."

"Hey!" says Avery. "It's so nice to meet you! I love your jeans!"

"And your shoes — super cute!" Bailey adds.

Alex grins and blushes. "Thanks!"

Madison just sits there quietly. I've told Alex all about Madison in our calls and texts, so hopefully the silence isn't a surprise.

Alex gives me a little nod, and I launch into her plan. "So I know Alex is only supposed to be staying two days, but we, uh, wondered if you guys would mind if she stayed a little longer." I pause. "Like maybe until Stefan's fashion show is done? Wednesday?"

I expect Bailey, Avery, and Madison to at least want to discuss it, but Avery just shrugs. "Fine by me. I told you this suite is roomy compared to what I'm used to."

"Same here," says Bailey. "We're always in and out anyway. Mallory Kane's show is tomorrow, so I won't be here a good part of the day."

"And Thomas Lord is Thursday," Avery adds, "so I'll probably be gone helping with some sort of prep on Monday and Tuesday."

Madison sighs and rolls her eyes. "Whatever. But she's going to be pretty bored while you're at work."

"Well, I've been doing research," says Alex, "and a lot of the Fashion Week websites I've looked at say designers are always looking for more volunteers. Is that true?"

Avery claps her hands. "Totally true! What an awesome idea! Why didn't I think of that earlier?"

"Do you think it'll be hard to clear with Stefan?" I ask.

"Doubt it," says Bailey, "but I'd ask first thing Monday morning. Don't wait until Wednesday."

Alex and I hug. "This will be so cool," I say. Then a thought comes to me. "But what about your plane ticket?"

"My dad made it open-ended. Once this is cleared, I'll call him, and he can confirm the departure date. Surprise!"

"I'm so jealous," says Avery, fake pouting. "I wish I'd thought of having a friend volunteer with me."

"It was all Alex's idea," I say with a grin. I'm so excited for her to see my designs and the world I've been living in for the past two months. Finally, I can share it with my best friend.

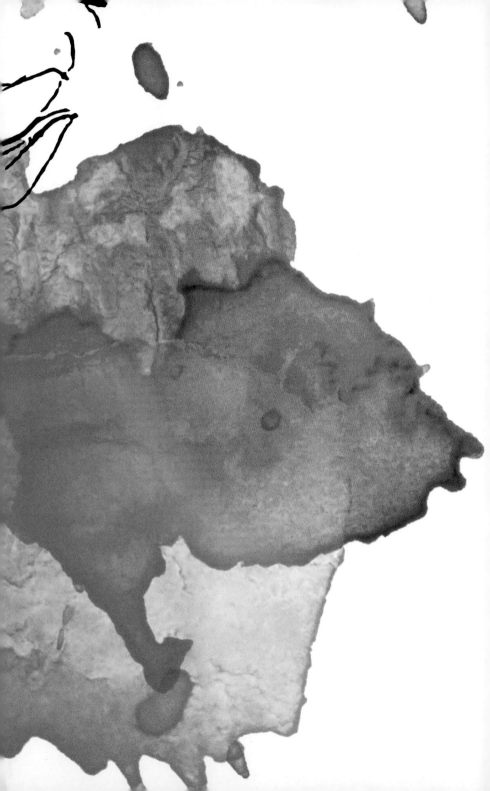

Alex and I are up extra early Monday morning, and I'm surprised by how excited my best friend is to put together her outfit. She pulls out a patterned blouse with a V-neck and pairs it with loose black shorts. Metallic flats complete the look.

I'm impressed. "I'm still surprised by this new Alex, but I so love it!"

Alex twirls in front of the mirror and bows dramatically. "Why, thank you, darling!"

I'd been thinking of wearing black shorts too, but I don't want us looking like twins, so instead I choose a short-sleeved lace blouse and pair it with taupe silk shorts and open-toed flats.

"I can't wait to see where you work," Alex says as we leave the dorm. "Let's just hope Stefan is looking for

volunteers. Maybe I should stay hidden until he says it's okay."

"Sounds like a plan," I say. I try to sound confident, but butterflies form in my stomach. What if he says no? We have almost an hour before the meeting starts. That will give Alex and me plenty of time to get to work and talk with Stefan, but that still doesn't totally quiet my butterflies.

* * *

When we get to the office, Stefan is setting up the meeting room. Alex hides behind the door, and I walk into the conference room.

"Early and eager," says Stefan, smiling. "I like that in an intern."

"Do you need help?" I ask.

"Why not? Please place a packet at everyone's seat," Stefan says, handing me a stack of papers.

I do as he says, but the butterflies are getting worse. "Um, Mr. Meyers?" I finally manage. "I was hoping to talk with you about something."

Stefan stops organizing and gives me his full attention. "What is it?" His face is serious.

"My friend Alex is visiting, and we were wondering if you could use more Fashion Week volunteers," I say. My heart is pounding, and I wring my fingers as I wait for him to answer.

Stefan breaks into a grin. "Is that all? I thought you were going to bail on me. We can always use more volunteers. I'm going over a lot of info at today's meeting. Can she get here?"

My face reddens. "Um . . . she's waiting outside."

Stefan laughs and peers out the door. "Ah, I see her. She's not a great hider, but at least she has style." He waves Alex into the room and extends his hand. "Stefan Meyers."

"Alex," she says. "I'm so excited to be here. Thank you for letting me help."

"If you're anything like your friend Chloe," says Stefan, "this will work out perfectly."

Alex and I finish passing out the packets as interns from all departments begin trickling in. When everyone is seated, Stefan begins his speech. "Tomorrow, I, along with the rest of the designers, will be busy with last-minute Fashion Week prep, so today is our last chance to talk at length before Wednesday's show," he says.

I'm sitting beside Alex and nudge her with my elbow. She grins. I know we're both jumping up and down on the inside.

Stefan starts off with a map of Lincoln Center and focuses on where our tent will be. Then he assigns our positions before, during, and after the show. Alex and I are responsible for placing the programs and gift bags on everyone's seats before the show begins. We'll also be assisting backstage with the models. I try to focus on what Stefan is saying even though my brain is turning cartwheels.

"Finally," he says, "a reminder. Your job is to assist with the Stefan Meyers brand. This is *not* a networking opportunity. This is *not* a time to tell other designers, editors, and critics how hard you've been working for me and which button was your design." He pauses and looks around the room. Is it my imagination, or do his eyes linger on Madison? "Believe me, I see your efforts. If you do what I ask of you, I'll notice. Questions?"

No one raises a hand.

"Excellent," Stefan says. "I expect to see you all at the tent by seven a.m. Wednesday. Remember to wear black, and don't forget to read through your packets. They also have your volunteer badges."

There are a few quiet groans about the early morning and the black. I don't know what the problem is. Early mornings are old news, and as for the black, it could be worse. Besides, it's Fashion Week! If Stefan said to wear a clown suit, I'd do it without complaints.

"Where to now?" asks Alex. "Can we scope out the tent for Wednesday?"

"Good idea," I say. As we get closer to Lincoln Center, the crowds thicken. Alex and I look at our maps and find Stefan's tent.

"Michael's description of it sounded great. I can't wait to see it!" I say as we duck inside. It's even better than I imagined. The white is simple yet elegant, and there's a humongous chandelier at the end of the runway, just like we'd discussed.

Alex whistles, impressed. "I love it. I was scared it would look crazy like some of those shows we watched online. Wasn't there a seal in one of them?"

I laugh. "Definitely no animals here."

We do a small tour of the space and check out the backstage area. "I can't believe we'll be a part of all this," says Alex.

"I know," I say. "I feel like I should pinch myself. I can't believe it's finally here."

* * *

That evening, Bailey tells us all about Mallory Kane's show. "It was super hectic," she says, "but amazing. I loved organizing all the outfits for the models and checking the guest list."

"I can't wait until Thursday's show!" Avery says.

"The end was really cool too," Bailey continues. "Mallory walked onstage after the last set of models, and everyone applauded. I was backstage, but all that energy was contagious. Even when I was cleaning up and packing up the clothes and extra gift bags and programs, I was so pumped. I just felt so good to be a part of the experience."

"That sounds amazing," I say. I close my eyes, picturing the lights and clothes on the runway.

"But we're not *really* a part of the experience," Madison says, cutting into my daydream.

"What do you mean?" asks Bailey.

Madison rolls her eyes. "I mean, we're just interns. You should have heard Stefan's speech this morning. He went on and on about how we need to focus on the Stefan Meyers brand. It's not about 'networking.'"

Bailey sighs. Her annoyed expression tells me she's had these conversations with Madison before. "You're there to help, not network. All the designers feel the same way about that. If you're being professional, you're asked to come back. Designers introduce themselves to you. There are opportunities."

"What do you think, Chloe?" Madison asks.

I glance back and forth between Bailey and Madison, not sure how to respond. I know if I agree with Madison, she might finally warm up to me. Although, the internship is almost over, so what does it matter? In a way, she has a point. I mean, who wouldn't want to talk to a famous designer or be the Cinderella of fashion?

But then I remember what Liesel and Laura said about things happening in their own time. I remember Gary saying there are more important things than seeing your name in lights. The truth is, regardless of how nice it would be to be the star of the show, tomorrow is about Stefan's brand and being a team player.

"I think our job is to just follow Stefan's directions," I finally say. "I wouldn't want to miss something important and be responsible for Stefan's show tanking."

Madison frowns. "Figures you wouldn't care about being heard, Diva Girl. You already had your moment in the spotlight."

"Hey!" says Alex. "Chloe worked really hard to get here."

"Forget it," I whisper.

Alex sputters like she wants to say something else but settles for glaring at Madison.

Madison gets up and heads to her room. "You guys do what you want, but I've worked too hard to be a wallflower. I'm not just going to sit back." She walks to her room, then turns around one last time. "Maybe I just want this more than the rest of you."

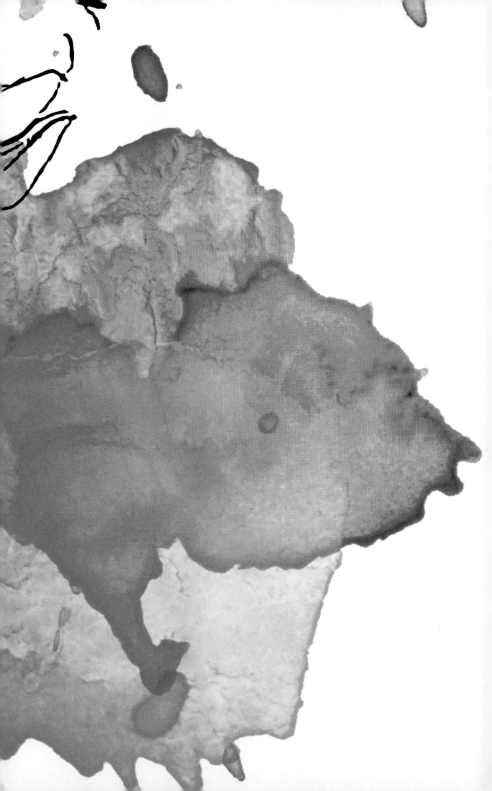

As soon as my alarm buzzes at six o'clock Wednesday morning, I jump out of bed. Alex, on the other hand, pulls the covers over her head and groans. That means I get the shower first, which is fine by me.

I quickly wash my hair and am finishing putting on my Fashion Week outfit — a black sheath dress, black tights, and black flats — when Alex starts banging on the door.

"Chill," I say, coming out. "I'm moving as fast as I can."

"Not my fault I can't function before eight. And factor in jet lag . . ." Eyes still half-closed, Alex pushes past me into the bathroom.

While she showers, I focus on doing my hair. I may not be able to spice up my wardrobe with some sparkle, but at least I can style my hair. I blow-dry it straight, then glance at the time on my phone — six-thirty. Good thing Alex's hair is shorter than mine and will require less styling, or we'd be late for sure.

When Alex finally emerges, she's wearing black flats too, but she's paired them with a black shift dress and tights with a zigzag pattern to keep us from looking identical.

"You look great!" I say, checking the time again.

Alex follows my gaze and pulls her hair back into a quick bun. "Not to worry," she says. "No dryer needed."

I smile, relaxing, and hook my arm through hers as we head out the door.

* * *

We get to Lincoln Center with five minutes to spare. Stefan has even set up an area with food and coffee.

"He's, like, the best boss ever," Alex chirps, helping herself to a bagel, eggs, bacon, and coffee.

I do the same, adding some fruit to my plate as well. It's going to be a long day, so I make sure to toss a couple protein bars and fruit in my bag for later.

I look around the room at the sea of black. Even with everyone dressed in the same color, it's amazing how much individuality there is. There are dresses with lace and ribbed and patterned tights. I see a few peplum dresses too, and spot one intern wearing a long black maxi, which I love. I could picture it spiced up with a statement necklace or scarf.

Stefan raises his hand for attention. "This is it," he says. "This is what we've been working toward. We're all here for the same purpose — to make sure the show runs smoothly."

Alex and I glance at Madison, but she appears to be very focused on her bagel.

"Work hard, have a good time. Any questions?" Stefan asks. The group is silent. "No? Then onward!"

Alex and I get right to work, grabbing a cart and loading the gift bags and programs onto it. My best friend and Fashion Week — what more could a girl ask for?

* * *

Alex and I place a program and gift bag on each seat in the tent, then step back to admire the whole thing once more. Even though we saw the finished product yesterday, it's more impressive today because of the energy. Volunteers are rushing from one station to another, Gary is doing sound checks, and models are being prepped.

"Girls," says Laura, rushing toward us. She's out of breath, as usual. "If you're done here, I need you backstage assisting with the models."

Alex and I exchange an excited look and follow Laura backstage into the chaos. Hairspray is being sprayed everywhere, shoes are being thrown from one direction to another, and stylists are doing last-minute dress adjustments.

"Where do you need us?" I ask.

"You'll help dress the models and keep track of the looks," says Laura. She hands us photos of the outfits the models will wear, along with the order they go in. "We have fifteen models and thirty looks. Each model will showcase two designs. You'll notice the first model will wear the first and last design on the list. There will be some time to change looks, but we need you girls to make the changes go as quickly as possible. If you need anything, ask the stylists, okay?"

We nod, and Laura runs off to assist someone else in need.

"Ten minutes!" a familiar voice yells.

I turn and spot Liesel off to the side. She's busy making last-minute adjustments to the pieces she and Taylor collaborated on. "Liesel!" I shout, running over to give her a hug.

She pauses long enough to hug me back. "This is it, Chloe! Are you ready?" she asks.

"Born ready," I say, chuckling. "You remember Alex, right?"

"Of course. Nice to see you again," says Liesel. "Excited to be here?"

"Totally! I can't believe I get to do this!" says Alex.

Liesel grins. "Me neither. It never gets old. We'll catch up after the show, okay? Best of luck!"

Liesel rushes toward Taylor and Stefan, who have just appeared backstage, and I help the first model into her outfit. It's the purple cotton dress with black trim Laura designed, based on my pockets.

"I love this one," says Alex, helping a model with a crochet tank dress. I recognize the scalloped hem and metallic threading.

"I helped Laura design that one," I say.

Alex whistles. "Mighty impressive, girl."

"Five minutes!" someone calls, and Alex and I stop chatting and focus on the task at hand.

I feel my heart beating quickly as the first models line up. We add pieces of adhesive tape and pins for last-minute fixes, and then they're ready. The music starts, and it's go time. This is it. It's happening.

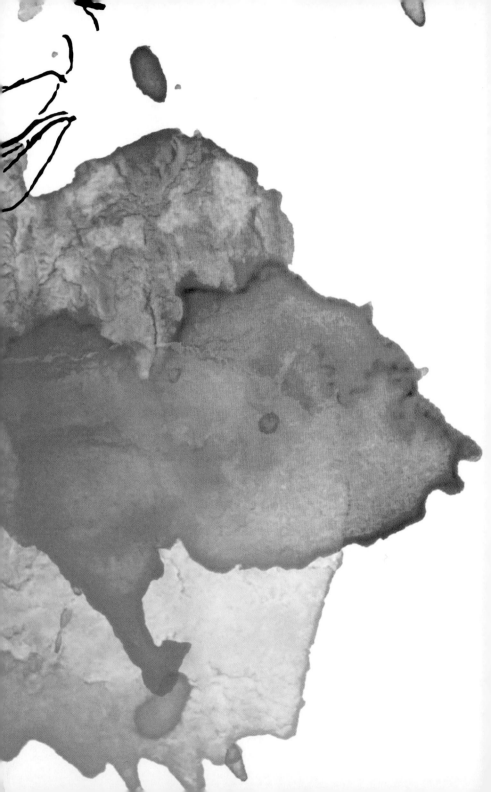

As the models hit the runway, Alex and I stay busy in the back, constantly checking Laura's list and comparing it with who's lined up to go. We have to make sure there isn't any lag time between one model and the next. That could throw off the whole show.

Even though I can't see the models on the runway, there's something amazing about seeing the designs on them backstage. The way fabric skims the hips or lays on the collarbone changes the garment, and I realize more than ever that there's a level of precision to choosing the right model to perfectly showcase a design.

It feels like we've been standing forever, and Alex and I make the mistake of sitting down just as the first models are strutting back in.

"Ladies!" yells Taylor. "Look alive!"

We jump up and rush to the models. The first fifteen looks were various knits and denims, and the last fifteen are all art deco themed. These are the pieces I've worked on with both Taylor and Laura.

A model lines up in a flowing, pleated yellow skirt and strapless bodice with shimmering geometric lines and metallic threading. I remember this design from my time with Taylor. I notice she's carrying a clam-shaped bag with white tile beads. That's the design I drew for Taylor! I remember her saying she'd pass it on to Stefan. Looks like he liked it. This is unreal. It's all I can do to focus and not scream with joy.

We move quickly, readying one design after the next. I smooth a jacket with a notched collar and beading that I recognize from my time with Laura. It fits beautifully over a satin gown embroidered with an overlapping V pattern that I helped Taylor with.

I scan the photos and list and see we're nearing the end. The dresses Liesel and Taylor worked on together are next. I help a model into a silk bias-cut gown, and a stylist adds a long pearl tassel necklace. I see Liesel putting the finishing touches on another model and give her a quick thumbs-up.

Out of the corner of my eye, I see Alex zipping a model into a rose-colored floor-length gown. The model twirls in the delicate chiffon, and I notice the beading

BEADED
HEADBAND

FINAL
FASHION WEEK
Design

FLOWY
PLEATED
SKIRT

BEADED &
CRYSTAL BODICE

ART DECO
BEADED
BAG

and sequin embellishments across the boat neckline. The dress is a lovely blend of vintage and glamour, and the embellishments perfectly capture the art deco vibe Stefan was going for with these pieces.

The model struts onto the runway. As breathtaking as the dress looked seconds ago, it's even better now. The chiffon flows behind the model, and the beading shimmers under the bright lights. The garment almost seems to come alive as the model floats down the catwalk.

"What do you think the chances are of us getting free samples of some of this stuff?" Alex asks as we put the next outfit on the model.

I laugh. "Doubtful — highly doubtful. It's a nice dream, though. I'd especially love this one," I say as I finish helping a model into a simple black satin dress with an art deco-inspired sash belt. I peer closer at the intricate pearl, crystal, and rhinestone detailing.

"Liesel is so skilled," says Alex. "No wonder she was a *Design Diva* winner! This will be you one day." She pokes me in the side.

"Here's hoping," I say, fastening the belt clasp.

I look at my list. One design left, and it's a total showstopper. I help the model into the silver beaded dress with a deep V-neck. The dress is held up by illusion-netting straps, giving it an ethereal look. The intricate beading design showcases Liesel's attention to detail. Unlike some of the other looks, this model's hair is pulled back in a bun, which adds to the style's sophistication. She walks onto the runway, the slinky dress hugging her hips.

Alex and I watch as the dress catches the light from the chandelier, eliciting gasps from the audience. I wipe a tear from my eye, and Alex pats my shoulder. "I feel like such an idiot for crying," I say. "This has just been such an amazing experience, and I can't believe it's almost over."

"I know. Getting to do this with you today was amazing. It makes me want to learn more about fashion too. You can really feel the dedication of all the designers today," says Alex. Her voice breaks, and she giggles. "Man, now you got me emotional. About clothes! Speak of this to no one."

I laugh. "Cross my heart."

The audience applauds for the final dress, and the model makes her return trip down the runway, heading toward the backstage area.

Now it's Stefan's turn to hit the catwalk. He has so much to be proud of today, but he's so humble as he walks out and waves to the audience, taking his time shaking their hands. He takes a final bow, and some of the audience members give him a standing ovation. As he makes his way off the stage, I see him wipe his eyes too.

BEADED COLLAR

PEARL TASSEL NECKLACE

BEADED BOATNECK GOWN

ART DECO PATTERN

ROSE-COLORED CHIFFON GOWN

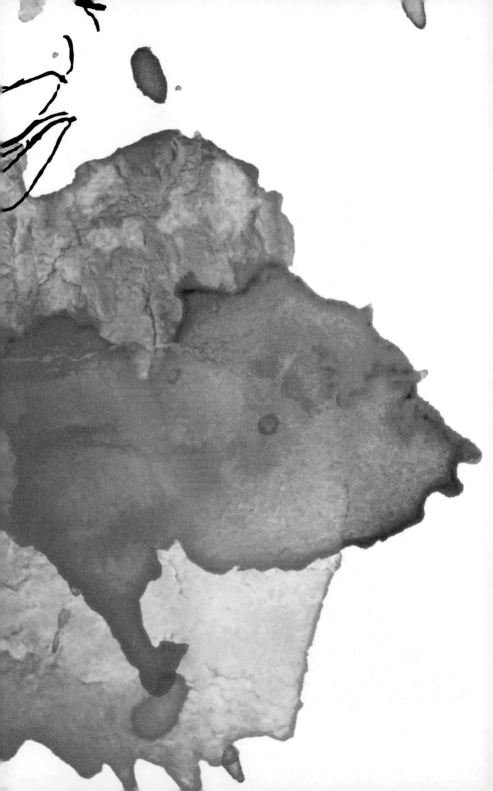

Still riding high after the end of the show, Alex and I leave the backstage area to see if help is needed out front. Some interns are picking up stray programs and gift bags, and we do the same. In the distance, I see Madison sitting by herself, head in her hands, shoulders shaking. She can't be this emotional over the fashion show, can she?

I poke Alex and nod in Madison's direction. "Do you think something happened?"

Alex shrugs and shakes her head. "Who knows? That girl is all drama."

I'm mentally debating whether or not I should check up on her when I hear a familiar voice yelling my name. I turn and see Jake hurrying toward me with a huge grin on his face.

"Hi!" I say, giving him a hug. It's been more than a week and a half since I last saw him, and I've missed him.

"Those designs were incredible," he says. "It must have been amazing seeing the final product after all the work you put in."

"It really was!" I say. "And the energy in the room was electrifying."

"I know!" Jake agrees. "My mom was able to get me a ticket, so I got to sit out front and watch the whole thing. I so lucked out." He waves Liesel over and puts his arm around her.

"I loved your designs," I say to Liesel. "The last piece was phenomenal."

Liesel smiles modestly. "Thank you. It was my favorite as well. And I'm so grateful to you and Alex for your help backstage. We couldn't have done it without you."

"Hey there," Jake says as Alex walks over. "I thought you looked familiar. Chloe's best friend from California, right? Good to see you again."

The three of them recap the show, and Alex gushes about the great time she had. I take it all in, trying not to think about how much I'll miss both Jake and Liesel when I head back to California this weekend.

Suddenly, I feel everyone staring at me. "Sorry, what? I zoned out."

Liesel smiles. "We were just saying how glad we were that we got to spend these months with you. We'll miss you, kiddo."

"Me too," I say, my eyes tearing up again.

"Don't worry," says Alex, throwing her arm around me. "I'll take care of her."

"And I'll be in Santa Cruz next month visiting my dad," says Jake. "I'll give you a call, and we'll hang out then, okay?"

"You'd better," I say. I hug him and Liesel one last time, then Alex and I finish cleaning up and head back to the dorms, leaving the glam of Fashion Week behind.

* * *

As soon as Alex and I walk in the door, Bailey is on us. "How was the show? Amazing? I've been dying to hear how it went."

"The best!" I say. "It was so cool seeing all the designs, especially the ones I got to help out with."

"I'm so excited for Thomas Lord's show tomorrow," Avery adds from where she's sitting. "But I'll be honest, I'm getting kind of sad too. Our time here is almost over. At least there's still the send-off."

I perk up. "Send-off?"

"Oh, yeah," says Bailey. "Most of the designers do a big breakfast on the last day for the interns. The lead designer comes and thanks everyone for all their hard work. Sometimes they even give you a gift."

"See?" says Alex. "I told you freebies were a possibility! And now that you have something to look forward to, you don't have to be gloomy after I leave." She winks at me.

I give her a half-hearted smile. "Too bad you can't be here for that," I say. Her flight back to California leaves tomorrow, and my last day as an intern is Friday.

Alex shrugs. "It's fine. This has been really exciting, and I wouldn't trade it for anything. I totally get why you love it here, but I'm really a Santa Cruz girl at heart. I don't think I can do the hustle and bustle thing on a daily basis."

"I can sympathize with that," says Bailey. "I miss my home in Florida too."

"Not me," says Avery, grinning. "My home is right here."

Alex throws a pillow at her and laughs.

"Hey," I say, just realizing Madison is missing in action, "do you know where Madison is? I saw her crying at Fashion Week."

Avery and Bailey exchange glances. "She *really* wanted to get noticed," Avery finally says with a shrug.

"What does that mean?" I ask. "What happened?"

"She tried to show Daphne Appell, that reality show host, some of her designs, and Daphne got annoyed. I guess her people complained to Stefan. It seems like it got blown out of proportion, at least according to Madison," says Bailey, sounding like she feels bad for even relating the story. "She was here earlier and said Stefan told her she can come to the breakfast Friday, but she can't intern for him again."

"Wow," says Alex. "If I were her, I wouldn't feel right going to the breakfast."

Avery shakes her head. "She won't. She's too embarrassed. She wants to change her ticket and leave Thursday."

Knowing Madison, she probably was a little pushy with Daphne, but I still feel bad. It stinks to go out on a sour note.

Suddenly, the door bursts open, and we jump. It's Madison, her face red and puffy. "Hi," she says quietly.

We look at her, unsure what to say.

Madison sighs. "I'm sure you told Miss Diva everything?"

"I'm really sorry," I say.

Madison snorts. "Yeah, well. Me too."

No one seems to know what to say, so Alex starts packing. The rest of us — except for Madison — try to help.

Finally, I can't take the awkwardness anymore. "You should stay until Friday," I finally say, breaking the silence. "Come to the breakfast. It was just a mistake."

Madison whips her head around, and I brace myself for some of her usual bad attitude, but she deflates. "It was a big one. I just — I just wanted someone to see my designs."

I nod. We all understand wanting recognition.

"Nothing I can do about it now," Madison says, heading to her room. "I might as well go home. But I'll say this, Diva Girl, one day you'll see my name plastered everywhere." She flashes a determined smile and disappears into her room.

I hope I do, I think. *I hope I see all our names plastered everywhere one day.*

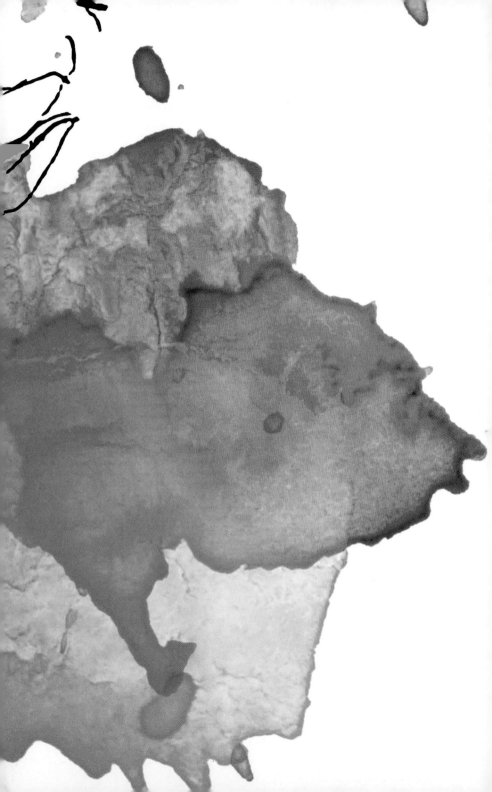

With Alex and Madison gone, Bailey, Avery, and I spend Thursday night packing. That way we can enjoy our last day and not feel pressured to get everything done before we leave Saturday.

And yet, when I wake up Friday morning, I find myself gloomy anyway. The day feels like a series of lasts. Last internship outfit, for example. Today, I'm wearing something I designed for my first *Design Diva* audition. It's a white dress with a cinched waist, full skirt, and leather accents at the shoulders. Perfect for a goodbye breakfast.

I head to the office for the last time and show Ken, the security guard, my badge.

"Have a great day, Miss Montgomery. It's been a pleasure," says Ken.

Sentimental girl that I am, my eyes start to water. I rush to the elevator, feeling silly, and take it up to the seventh floor — where it all began.

I step off the elevator and look around, remembering when Laura first gave me a tour. I look at designers working on prototypes and samples and think about the pockets I made. Someone is pinning a dress to a mannequin, and I envision the dresses I made for Taylor. I close my eyes, holding all the moments in my mind. From organizing the closet, to lugging clothes to *Vogue*, to confirming interviews for Michael, to working with models — it's all been a dream come true.

The conference room is filled with interns, all eating and chatting, when I walk in. I see Laura, Stefan, and Taylor in a corner talking with a group of interns and head to the food table to grab something to eat. I pile a bagel, eggs, fruit, and bacon onto my plate and grab a juice with my other hand, carefully carrying the items to the conference table.

"That takes some serious skill," Laura says, sliding into the seat next to me. "I was just thinking about our first meeting and my coffee-stained skirt."

I laugh. "I forgot about that. Your skirt — not the meeting."

"It feels like it was yesterday," Laura says. "I'm really going to miss having you here."

"Me too. You've taught me so much. Not only about fashion but also about how to act in this business. I'll never forget your support."

Now Laura looks choked up. She gives me a hug. "Chloe, it's been such a pleasure working with someone who's not only talented but works so hard. I know you want to be noticed. When your time comes, I'll be right there cheering you on."

"Talking to our Diva Girl?" says Stefan.

I look up, surprised. When Madison called me that, it sounded like the world's worst insult. When Stefan says it, it sounds like a compliment.

"Yes, sir," says Laura. "Just telling Chloe how much we'll miss her."

"Laura's right. You've shown a lot of promise," says Stefan. "I'd love to have you back next summer."

"I'm here if you'll have me!" I exclaim, almost knocking over my juice in excitement.

"We'd better step back when we give her the gift," Taylor says, coming up behind me. "She might jump out of her seat and spill her food on us."

I blush, but I know Taylor is just teasing. "I don't need a gift," I say. "My time here has been enough."

"Please," says Laura, waving away my words. "Ah, there's Michael. He has it."

I turn my head quickly. My time here *has* been the best gift ever, but I'd be lying if I said I wasn't intrigued by Michael's gift bag.

"Here she is," he says, handing me a black bag stuffed with silver paper. "Hope you like it."

I look around to see the other interns holding gift bags too and looking at the contents. I push the paper aside and see a Stefan Meyers gift card tucked inside.

"Oh wow!" I exclaim. "This is awesome!"

"I like my interns showing off my looks. I need all the exposure I can get," says Stefan, winking. "Buy yourself some chic back-to-school wear."

This takes back-to-school shopping to a whole new level! I picture myself in some of my favorite Stefan Meyers styles. A white sweater dress spruced up with bangle bracelets and layered with necklaces. Or maybe I'll start the year in a black ruffled skirt, knit top, and printed scarf. For a cooler day, I might go for a gray knitted pendulum sweater with stylish black boots. This gift card opens up so many possibilities!

"I think we've lost her," says Laura.

I blush. I got so caught up in my new-outfit fantasy, I forgot to say thank you. "Oh my gosh, thanks so much. This is way too generous."

"There's more," says Taylor.

I look inside and gasp. It's the frayed pair of jeans I saw my first day in the closet, but that's not what makes me gasp — it's the back pockets. They're the pockets I helped design. And on the back of the pockets, where the Stefan Meyers logo normally is, someone stitched a circle with my initials intertwined — my very own CM logo.

"Remember when I told you one day you'll have your own intern and stores filled with the CM label?" asks Laura.

I nod. That was way back at the end of my second week.

"This is a start," says Laura, grinning.

"You guys, this is just amazing. I have no words," I say.

"We wanted to do something special for you," Taylor says. "Your very first CM original."

I hug the jeans to me. This is better than my name in lights.

* * *

When the breakfast is done, I finish saying my goodbyes and head back to my dorm room, walking slowly and taking in my last full day in the city.

I think about how much has changed in the past three months. What was I looking for when I auditioned for *Design Diva*? I imagined fame. I hoped for my designs to become well known. Then I won the internship, and it was as if my dreams were coming true. But I realized it was about more than recognition.

This has been such a journey. I thought I knew how everything worked, and now I know there's still so much more to learn. Even if I get to be as successful as Stefan, there's more to learn.

I take the subway to Bryant Park. I remember how the subway used to scare me. It seemed so confusing at first with all the routes laid out in different colors. Now hopping on the train feels like second nature.

At the park, I walk past the tables where Alex and I played Jenga. I think about what she said before she left: "I'm still a Santa Cruz girl at heart."

I used to think I was too. Now I'm not so sure. I listen to the honking horns and fire sirens outside the park. I look at the crowds of people and vendors. Each area of sidewalk is covered with people or stands. I find an empty bench and take out my sketchpad.

Today, I don't focus on just one person. I try to capture as many looks as I can. I draw a girl in cropped pants and lace-up oxfords with large gold hoops in her ears. I shade in the checkered pattern of another woman's minidress, then focus on her beige wedge sandals laced up the calf. A teenaged boy in jeans and a polo shirt throws a Frisbee to his friend. I notice the Stefan Meyers logo on the boy's jeans and think of the gift Laura, Taylor, Michael, and Stefan made me. Someday people in this park will be wearing jeans with the CM logo.

I go back to the sketches I just drew and add the CM logo to the pieces. This year will be all about adding to my CM brand. That, and learning how to make my designs crisper. And when I see Stefan again next summer, he'll see how far this California girl has come.

KNIT TOP &
PRINTED SCARF

KNIT PENDULUM
SWEATER

SM
JEANS!

GOLD!

WHITE
SWEATER
DRESS

BLACK RUFFLED
SKIRT

SM INTERN
GIFT CARD
Sketches

CM Logo
on
Back Pocket!!

The Author

Margaret Gurevich has wanted to be a writer since second grade and has written for many magazines, including *Girls' Life*, *SELF*, and *Ladies' Home Journal*. Her first young adult novel, *Inconvenient*, was a Sydney Taylor Notable Book for Teens, and her second novel, *Pieces of Us*, garnered positive reviews from *Kirkus*, *VOYA*, and *Publishers Weekly*, which called it "painfully believable." When not writing, Margaret enjoys hiking, cooking, reading, watching too much television, and spending time with her husband and son.

The Illustrator

Brooke Hagel is a fashion illustrator based in New York City. While studying fashion design at the Fashion Institute of Technology, she began her career as an intern, working in the wardrobe department of *Sex and the City*, the design studios of Cynthia Rowley, and the production offices of *Saturday Night Live*. After graduating, Brooke began designing and styling for Hearst Magazines, contributing to *Harper's Bazaar*, *House Beautiful*, *Seventeen*, and *Esquire*. Brooke is now a successful illustrator with clients including *Vogue*, *Teen Vogue*, *InStyle*, Dior, Brian Atwood, Hugo Boss, Barbie, Gap, and Neutrogena.

FOLLOW CHLOE'S *DESIGN DIVA* JOURNEY FROM THE BEGINNING!

www.capstoneyoungreaders.com

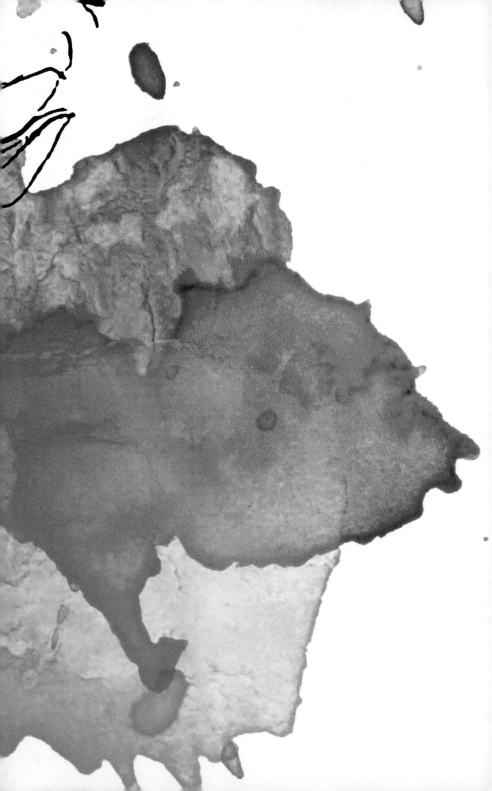